ECHOES

in the

FOG

Literary Reflections on the Liminal Spaces of Maine's Coast

INTRODUCTION BY ROBIN ALDEN | EDITED BY STEVEN LONG

Cover Illustration and Map: Dan Kirchoff | www.dankirchoff.com
Interior Formatting and Cover Design: Mariella Travis | www.alleiram.com
eBook Conversion: Sam Sheng | linkedin.com/in/samsheng

ISBN
978-1-961905-70-2 (Paperback)
978-1-961905-71-9 (eBook)

12 Willows Press
Winterport, Maine
www.12willowspress.com

TABLE OF CONTENTS

ACKNOWLEDGMENTS

"A Light at the End" by Kristen Lindquist was previously published in *Drifting Sands Haibun*, vol. 23 (September 2023).

"A Rogue Wave" by Richard Foerster was previously published in his *Trillium* (BOA Editions, Ltd., 1998).

"A Shoal" by Richard Foerster was previously published in his *River Road* (Texas Review Press, 2015).

"Channel Black" by Valerie Lawson was previously published in *Flyway: Journal of Writing and Environment* (Spring 2026).

"counting steps in fog" by faith lane was previously published in her *lighthouses of midcoast maine & tales of the folk who lived there* (2024).

"Dreams of Drowning" by Kristen Lindquist was previously published in *Contemporary Haibun Online*, vol. 19.1 (Spring 2023).

"From Right Here, in the Salt Wind" by Patricia Smith Ranzoni was previously published in her *Hibernaculum & Other North-Natured Poems* (Onewater Press, 2010).

"Journey of the Swim, or Cannery: A Parable of Reproduction" by Jefferson Navicky was previously published in *The Paper Coast* (Spuyten Duyvil, 2018) and in his *The Catch: Writings from Downeast Maine*, vol. 4 (2016).

"Salt Dawn" by Patricia Smith Ranzoni was previously published in her *SETTLING: Poems* (Puckerbrush Press, 2000).

"Spring Tide" by Richard Foerster was previously published in his *Patterns of Descent* (Orchises Press, 1993).

The stanza "dissolving fog" in "For: Haiku" by Catherine J.S. Lee was previously published in *Shamrock Haiku Journal* (Fall 2010).

The stanza "summer night" in "Fog: Haiku" by Catherine J.S. Lee was previously published in *A New Resonance 7: Emerging Voices in English Language Haiku* (Red Moon Press, 2021) and in her *All That Remains: A Haiku Collection Inspired by a Maine Childhood* (Turtle Light Press, 2010/Sea Smoke Press, 2018).

The stanza "tendrils of fog" in "Fog: Haiku" by Catherine J.S. Lee was previously published in *The Aurorean* (Spring-Summer 2008)

"Washed Up" by Kristen Lindquist was previously published in her *Island* (Red Moon Press, 2023).

"Windeyes" by Patricia Smith Ranzoni was previously published in *Heartbeat of New England: An Anthology of Contemporary Nature Poetry* (Tiger Moon, 2000) and her *Hibernaculum & Other North-Natured Poems* (Onewater Press, 2010).

EDITOR'S NOTE

Steven Long

Maine's coastline stretches 230 miles. But when every bay, inlet, and tidal river is counted, it runs nearly 3,480 miles, with more than 4,600 islands scattered offshore. For thousands of years, people have called this coast home. The "Red Paint" people, named for the red clay that lined the graves of their dead, settled here some 5,000 years ago. Dozens of tribes followed, though today only the Mi'kmaq, Penobscot, Passamaquoddy, and Maliseet remain. Later, Europeans arrived, drawn to the vast forests that supplied masts and timber for shipbuilding, as well as to the coastal waters, estuaries, and rivers teeming with fish and shellfish.

That spirit lives in this anthology. *Echoes in the Fog: Literary Reflections on the Liminal Spaces of Maine's Coast* brings together 58 contributors, including poets, short story writers, essayists, and photographers, each capturing the shifting moods of the shoreline and sea. My thanks go to Robin Alden for her introduction, Annaliese Jakimides for editorial guidance, Dan Kirchoff for the cover illustration and map, and Mariella Travis for the book's design.

Like the two previous anthologies in this series, $1 from every sale will be given to a Maine-based conservation nonprofit. For *Echoes in the Fog*, we've chosen the Maine Coast Heritage Trust, whose work safeguards the beauty and vitality of Maine's ever-changing coast.

When my wife and I first moved to Maine, we lived in Stockton Springs, overlooking Penobscot Bay, before settling in Winterport. Having grown up in western Kansas and spending my early years in the Midwest, I wasn't prepared for the fog that rolled in from the bay. On early morning walks, it transformed the familiar into something mystical and ethereal, and inevitably set my imagination ablaze. May this anthology do the same for you.

INTRODUCTION

Robin Alden

Echoes in the fog ...

This collection takes us there—into the fog—with all its mystery, disorientation, and wonder. The writing and photography here explore a spectrum that ranges from sinister to breathtakingly beautiful.

An artist friend once told me, after taking a workshop on painting fog, "Always use three colors to make the gray." What richness lies within that simple cloud, the mists of time suspended in each droplet. When we can't see with our eyes, when sound is distorted and direction confused, when scents drift disembodied—we are forced to rely on senses we seldom use. The smell of a raspberry meadow on an unseen island or herring in the water can be so unfamiliar that at first we can't even identify them. In fog, we are thrown into ourselves.

This anthology primarily focuses on ocean fog, or more simply, encounters with the ocean itself. It's only a small leap from the interiority that fog elicits to the ocean's own mysteries. Like fog, the ocean is alien to most land-dwellers. We look out across the surface, but the life below remains hidden.

So too, ocean issues are often out of sight and out of mind. For more than fifty years, I've worked for sustainable fisheries, trying to understand how Maine communities can live from the ocean by staying within its means. This is a challenge that requires learning not only about the ocean but also about ourselves and the ways we form responsible communities.

Humans are clever, and in the last half-century, we've undeniably "won the war against fish." Our technology is now so powerful that we can no longer delude ourselves. We can overfish. We can even alter the marine system itself.

Two innovations in particular—radar and positioning electronics such as GPS—have transformed our relationship with the sea. Radar allows fishermen, yachtsmen, and boaters to "see" in the fog, while GPS enables precise returns to the same spot in the vast ocean, to a treasured fishing ground, or to retrieve nets or lobster traps.

My husband, Ted Ames, grew up on Vinalhaven in the 1940s and early 1950s, when none of those tools were available. Fishing meant using compass navigation and running time. In a fog mull, the only additional "data" besides your watch and compass card came from smell, taste, and sound. The scent of bayberry from an island meadow or the smell of whales, something you might have overlooked if your senses were not on overdrive. The unmistakable signal from flats at low tide, or car exhaust from the mainland, registers more as taste than smell. And the sound—the toll of a buoy bell or the sudden whoosh of a kelp ledge when your course, running time, or compensation for wind, tide, and current was slightly off.

The coast had more fog then than it has had in the last ten years. Weeks could pass with fog that was, indeed, pea soup, with no clearing during the heat of the day. Ashore, the buildings across the street merely loomed, and droplets fell from phone wires, tree branches, flowers in the garden—even from your nose. On the water, the fog enveloped you; no side, no up, no forward or back. You were socked in. Dungeon-thick-a-fog.

Ted once went out to haul his traps on such a day, working them around the ledges and shoals of bordering islands. By midafternoon, he returned pleased that he'd found and hauled every one. His grandfather, a retired lighthouse keeper and fisherman, was not as pleased. "Don't do that again, Ted," he cautioned. "Most people don't haul on days like this. If you do, people will start thinking you're out there hauling their traps."

That concern has diminished with the advent of modern electronics. Today, many lobstermen are "out to haul" even in the thickest fog. Technology has expanded the human footprint on the ocean, both in time and geography. Side-scan sonar now renders the bottom almost literally—like a high-definition video game—down to the individual boulder, while simultaneously displaying the gear itself. Some say it has "taken the brains out" of fishing.

This marks a notable change from my tenure as Maine commissioner of marine resources in the 1990s. Then, I used a simple guideline to judge proposed regulations. I tried to make rules that benefited skill over capital because technology, when left unchecked, can overwhelm resources and concentrate fishing revenues in the hands of a few. My goal was to preserve a distributed, small-scale fishery that contributed to the entire coast of Maine. Today, even small-scale fishing operations are dominated by these high-tech tools.

So how do we find balance in our use of the Gulf of Maine so that Maine communities can continue to live from the ocean's bounty, whatever it produces?

The Gulf is vast—complex, dynamic, and challenging to understand. Yet the job of a fishery manager is to know enough to make informed decisions for human society, which is itself complex and ever-changing, while using the Gulf's resources without causing harm. This is a stunningly ambitious goal: not simply siting a business in or on the ocean, but using its productivity while operating within its means. Like navigating in a fog mull, achieving this requires many ways of knowing.

Since the 1970s, federal fisheries regulation has relied on an approach called scientific fisheries management. Its principal tool is counting fish: for example, assessing the number of cod in the Gulf of Maine and setting a quota for the entire area. This quantitative method is based on a 1950s population dynamics model: regulating the number of fish that fishermen catch directly impacts the size of the future population.

Unfortunately, that direct relationship has never been demonstrated. And tragically, this approach has been disastrous for Gulf of Maine groundfish stocks and for Maine fishermen. Today, Maine catches less than 1 percent of the cod it landed in 1977, the year the law passed. Cod collapsed in eastern Maine in the mid-1990s and has not rebuilt.

Nonetheless, this quantitative approach is not only codified in law but also attractive to both the federal government and the environmental community because it appears to create accountability. It has even been applied to social science, seeking the "optimal" number of fishermen to harvest the quota—called rationalization. A market mechanism known as catch shares privatized the fishery by giving boat owners a percentage of the total quota, based on how much each boat had caught during specific past years. For cod, those shares have since been bought, sold, and consolidated so that now fishing rights for cod and other groundfish are concentrated in New Bedford,

Massachusetts. There, fishermen work as sharecroppers for companies that own both the scarce federal groundfish permits and the catch shares.

Sight is still useful in a fog mull, just as counting fish remains important in fisheries management. But navigation in fog also depends on sound, smell, and even taste—and fisheries too require many other ways of knowing: not only how many fish are caught, but how, when, and where. Recognizing the complexity of the marine system is paramount.

Happily, the same technology that has intensified fishing has also contributed to an explosion of marine science, progressing far beyond simply counting fish. We now understand major current patterns in the Gulf and can track shifting bottom temperatures, plankton blooms, and the influence of both the Gulf Stream and Arctic meltwater. We know the Gulf is warming with climate change, but the warming is nuanced, differs from place to place, and ebbs and flows.

We know far more about fish life stages and the conditions for larval survival. Cod, for example, form small, place-specific subpopulations and, like salmon, return to their spawning grounds with amazing precision. Young fish learn migratory foraging routes from older fish—helping explain why small subpopulations, such as the one extinguished from Penobscot Bay in the 1990s, may not rebuild once overfished.

We also recognize the vital connection between the marine and river systems. Coalitions of fishermen, state agencies, community activists, environmental groups, and scientists are removing dams and rebuilding fish passage for species like river herring—the alewives and bluebacks that spawn in fresh water and live in the ocean. These fish are rebounding in astounding numbers throughout the state, restoring the vital nutrient flow between inland waters and the sea.

In the past fifty years, the formal study of complex systems that arose from computer science has moved into socio-ecological systems such as fisheries. The lesson is clear: the best strategy is to learn and adapt constantly, at multiple scales, just as one adjusts course in a fog based on new input from many senses. Elinor Ostrom's Nobel Prize-winning work on comanagement in resource industries, including the successful Maine lobster fishery, demonstrated the strength of responsibility and observation by those who work the resource.

Maine is well on the way to practicing this approach. The most visible example is its lobster rules, which avoid the quota system in favor of preserving critical life stages like juveniles and breeders, limiting technology and mobility, and requiring apprenticeship rather than capital for entry. Maine fishermen are engaged in stewardship and science in lobster, as well as in inshore scallops, clams, halibut, and alewives. We need all our senses, all disciplines—from fishermen observing daily in countless coves and bays, to the marine science community, regulators, and marine patrol who keep the system fair, to the nonprofits that knit these pieces together. There is no one quantitative solution, only the Maine community muddling through to feed itself and the world.

The Gulf of Maine is changing as it always has. With climate change, the pace has quickened, and we now perceive it more clearly. It piques our interest, yet the ocean remains a mysterious entity, and our understanding of it is limited. This is a time to navigate as if in a fog mull, using all our collective senses and expertise, while also being attuned to our inner selves. Then we can push the tiller or turn the wheel, taking constructive action as best we can, adjusting as our shared observations demand. In this way, we may fish forever, right here, from our own communities.

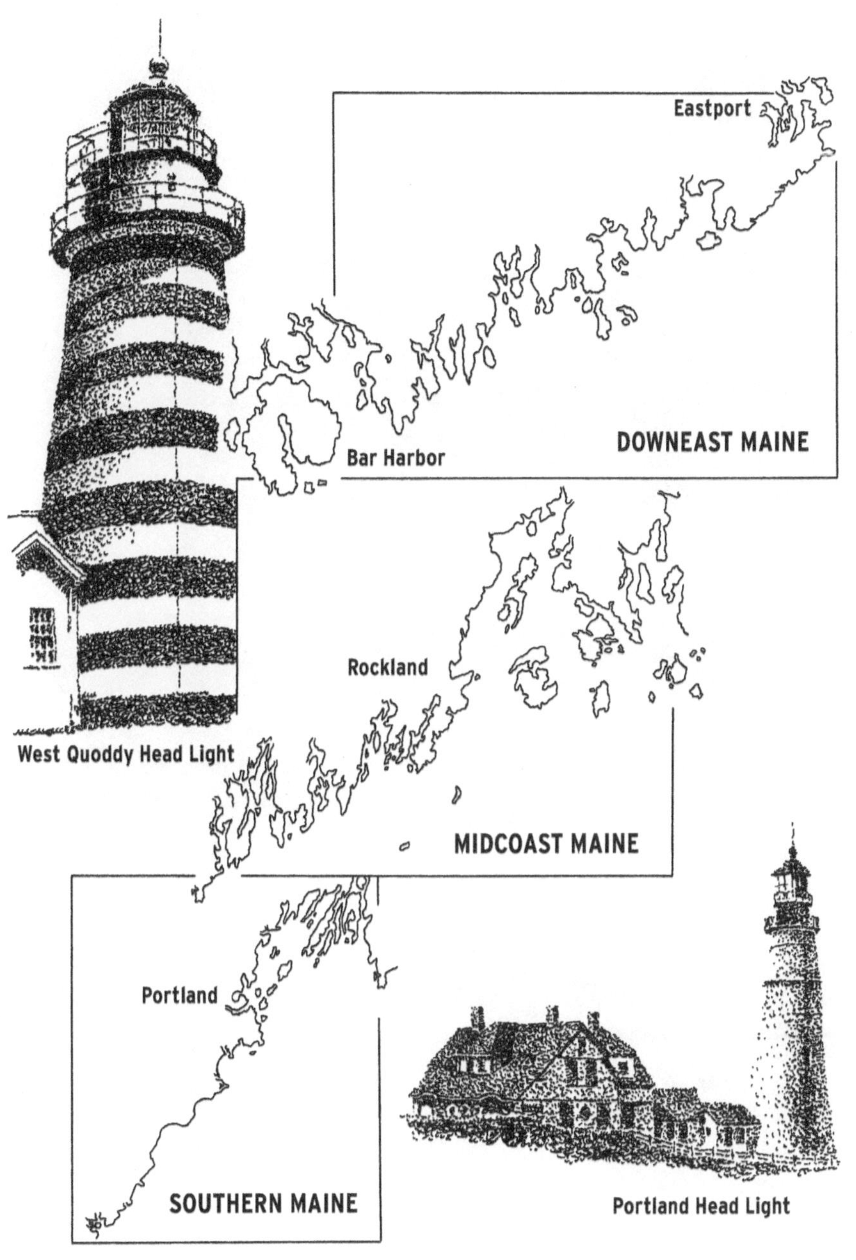

MAP OF THE MAINE COAST

Dan Kirchoff

THE VOICE OF THE BAY

William Henry Forester

The fog comes without a sound,
rolling in from the open sea,
settling low over the harbor
like something ancient, something watching.
It moves between the pilings,
brushes against the hulls of boats
that have not left their moorings in years.
The tide carries it inward,
up the river mouth,
through the reeds,
over the stones still slick with memory.
A bell rings from somewhere unseen—
distant, deliberate.
A call, or perhaps an answer.
Or perhaps just the weight of things
that cannot be spoken aloud.
A gull lifts into the thickened air,
a brief shape,
its cry swallowed before it can be heard.
The water shifts below, restless,
but the land holds still, waiting.
Everything here listens.

THERE WILL BE FOG

Valerie Lawson

They say the foggiest place in Maine,
Moose Peak Light on Mistake Island,
lies just off the coast of Jonesport.
Or maybe it's Little River Light in Cutler
or West Quoddy Head in Lubec.

Fog makes everything relative—
foreground and background dissolve,
channel markers and buoys disappear.
You can talk about conditions, the season,
but there's one thing you can count on:
there will be fog. Nets tangle. Traps get lost.
That was three things. And so many more ways for trouble.

Prepare all you want, shit's gonna happen.
But there's one thing you can count on: the heartbeat sound
of the foghorn and the bright beam of light—the long arms
of the lighthouse reaching out bringing the fisherman home.

"Liminal" by Lisa Tyson Ennis

DECIPHERING SAND, DECIPHERING WATER

Marcia F. Brown

Three white-tailed deer cantered here,
wove a cloven helix
in the sand, just above

the quick, incoming tide.
I suspect they felt deep in their withers,
my approaching steps,

made for the far end of the beach,
stag-leaping mutely
into the dunes.

This day is already ephemeral—
low waves running out
over the worn stones,

bearing their cargos of tiny life.
Light wind of purest oxygen
tugs the tethered life in me

up, up. I'm glad
the deer ran off, leaving me
to imagine the elegant arcs

of their morning run: pale sun
on pale flanks. Invisible too
are the blue and granite-grained fish,

weaving through curtains
of seaweed, to the wet shoals,
to the fathomless and beyond—

to the line of water-air
where motion meets vast stillness.
And what I know was here

just minutes ago—just yesterday, it seems—
calls to me in your voice
that I know better than my own,

entreating me to decipher
what I cannot see, to lift
out of the wet sand, out of the water,

what on earth has happened
and goes on happening here—
where we walked—just so,

on this sand. Then never again.
And even you, who would give me anything
you could, cannot turn to me

with some breath of comfort.
There is so much silence
and so much room for invention

when we become our absences, leaving
tracks like intricate hieroglyphs
on the shimmering, trammeled world.

A LIGHT AT THE END

Kristen Lindquist

of a granite jetty a mile out into the harbor, often cut off from land during a storm or full moon high tide. The lightkeeper's house long empty, its ceiling slumping above stained and peeling wallpaper. No furniture left. Plumbing disconnected. Walls as full of rats as the hold of an old ship. Yet over the musty kitchen sink out of use for forty, fifty years, one window frames open ocean. Just water and sky, islands on the distant horizon. A small flock of eiders flies past, out to sea. I'm thinking of the keeper's wife.

sea smoke
sheltering
in plain sight

COUNTING STEPS IN FOG

faith lane

thirty-three steps
to the barn for chores
twenty-two steps to the bell
to peal the warning
more steps in either direction
leads into the woods
toward the brook

fifty-eight steps to the tower
if you counted that
but could not see
or touch the tower
you were off course
possibly lost

one hundred twenty-seven steps to the top of the tower
to the light
to shine a warning or a welcome

seventy-five? eighty?
steps to cliff's edge

GHOST SPRUCES

Kate Kearns

Calcified to bone,

their pins
long dropped,

a host of spruces
guards
the coastline.

Air, brittle light,

go right through—
sharpen them

to Neptune's toothpicks.

Branches endure
in line
with the wind

stripped of color,
of sap,

down to the essential
core,
harsh and eternal.

Peace, a silver
arrow

embedded
in moss,

more stone than stone.

JULY DESIRE PATH, COD COVE

Jennie Kuhn

On July's sudden threshold,
Cod Cove fever found us,
heels sinking into thirsty curves
of grit-dappled dunes.
Prostrate, we prayed,
stretched flat like oarweed frond,
taut seabelt;
lion's mane tangled and untangled.
We stayed, watched in awe,
the unbaptized children of ellipsis,
of tectonic collision.
We met water's edge,
embroidered with fickle seafoam,
and followed resonant voices
on salt-beckoning wind,
asking, between
the thunder of jetty crash,
the moan of tide sharp
against beach rubble,
"Do you yearn?"
Part of me stayed ankle-caught
in steep crevice—
marooned there, somewhere
on your jagged continuum of breath.

Heartbeats swift, like sandpiper feet or
gull shriek, or swift how sunset begins
and ends, or maybe like Luna moth gasp,
I chased you then, tugged from June,
like some spinning kite,
unruly, windstrewn,
lingering in loose witchgrass,
our faces cool under sweet cloud shadow.
We spun cashmere daydreams between fingers
sticky with sugar-kelp, taking shelter from
the bellowing lungs of distant thunderheads.

We return, seeking
the forgiveness of sea breeze,
sand-soft skin, pockets heavy with
smooth stones. Brittle parts of us scuttle
between mass strandings of driftwood,
scattered tree ribs, barnacles.
Flutter of narrow tern, we listen,
waiting for the honeyed mercies
to find us again.

Even now, I pace the desire path
between our silences—
yours and mine.
I pursue, yet
ignis fatuus,
you retreat,
ebb tide,
vanish into that stillness
where no part of me
can follow.

AT THE EDGE OF THE WORLD

Kathleen Ellis

Here, where the land meets water,
it drops off
precipitously, as if
the continent's outer crust
has something to prove.

And we have moved
to this border
of ourselves, stalwart
yet slightly unwelcome
from another coast,
to the easternmost town
in America.

And someone asks
if we have a *bot*.
Not what you're thinking—
but a *boat*.
(The long *oh*)
We say *No,*
but we have a kayak.

The someone decides
to like us anyway,
even if we don't speak
the same dialect.

On this shingle beach,
I ask the ocean what it thinks,
and it answers
in a rat-a-tat clattering
of stones.

BAR ISLAND SWIM

Ron Beard

Scores of students at College of the Atlantic in Bar Harbor plunge into the ocean for the annual swim from the Bar Island sandbar back to the school dock on Eden Street. The water temperature was near the seasonal high at 55 degrees.
—Mount Desert Islander, *September 17, 2015*

With the plunge, paralysis
memory triggers arms legs lungs
flailing limbs fail to find traction—
a ship whose propellers are turning but is yet underway—
struggling to slow panicked breath
      you set your bearings.

Self-preservation gives way to determination
for the arc of the undertaking
one shore falls away, the other looms
dancing between gravity and buoyancy
muscles and breath in synchrony
stubborn fears ease
as you swim into one slender sun-warmed current
snaking along the shore
finally grasping the rung of the ladder
hauling out like a walrus
shaky limbed walk
      towards blue towels and hot tea.

Each year we dive to recover the truth
rescuing challenge from preambles and protocols—
jumbled lecture on hypothermia (five warning signs)
waved waivers
          long march against honking traffic.

Giddy chatter propels us to the gravel bar
laid bare by receding tide
painting by Seurat:
          tourists stroll, dogs bark, gulls wheel
          kayak guides gather their flocks
          who trundle with double-ended paddles
          and waterproof bibs to plastic boats—
          small yellow whales beached and bleached and waiting.

At the end of the bar, two white vans—
the first with the symbol of the college that opens
its year with this swim, the meaning of the hieroglyph
lost to all but the first class;
a SWAT team flanks the other
stern rangers in dark glasses, perhaps assembled
to make sure we don't make a break
for Gouldsboro's forested islands
          or the bay beyond.

On the sloping shore a rope fence looped
slender stakes driven into the shingle.
We line up
we sign the memory book
maintained over a quarter century
we surrender our valuables
perhaps to be returned if we make it to the far shore.
A cheerful staff member checks our name
another inks a number on our upper arm.

Save these tattoos, to identify us should we fail to float
we are now nearly naked, edging toward the water
we try not to be conscious of our own bodies
        though conscious of the bodies of others.

We are all shapes, sizes, ages, hues
refugees herded together in a corral
to swim a third of a mile to freedom.
I chat with a woman whose name
I cannot remember, but whose eyes are kind.
Some swimmers have flippers, wet-suit tops
others clad in bikinis or baggy trunks, or not at all.
Nervous talk and bravado hides hesitation.
Three foghorn blasts from the watchboat *Osprey*
we stumble tender-footed over barnacle-crusted cobbles
        splashing into body-numbing water.

Out from shore, I look back:
one hundred and more bobbing heads
like a rookery of seals swimming west
to the distant dock hidden
in the glare of the setting sun
swimming in order to tell the story
        swimming to claim their future.

JOURNEY OF THE SWIM, OR CANNERY: A PARABLE OF REPRODUCTION

Jefferson Navicky

May we be blessed by
the spirits of these fish
—Gary Lawless, "Sardine Songs"

Such things only happen in the summer up here. They'd closed it up for good some time ago. But that just opened it for a different kind of commerce. He was up from down south, kept making his way north, farther and farther, a drifter, a musician who went by the name of Brother Adam, but who wasn't really a musician, only told people that, more of a drifter with a harmonica to fit the image.

With a snap, a pry, and a squeeze, he was in. Stale air layered above the forever linger of fish. He didn't mind. Never did. You go on and live with it. Tell you one thing, he ain't gonna change much. He settled in. As much as ever. The air seemed to pass through his hollowed mind, not an easy feat, but he'd done it through roads and time. He hid it all in his big, bushy white beard, and after enough years, beard absorbed it, took him in, and left him there with pleasant eyes of a pale shade.

He moved around. This took a few weeks. His portly form, recognized around town, got called "Gandalf" a few times by some punk kids. Fine, let them laugh, "Fat Gandalf." Indeed, harrumph. Whatever.

He came home at night, careful not to shine lights too obvious in the fishery windows. Took to eating sardines with fingers, in honor of his surroundings, an offering to the fishery gods of the past, bit of a sacrifice at first, then he grew to like them. And of course, those little fishies cheap, yeah. Got them at the dollar store where everything except sardines is more than a dollar, seventy-five cents, as they should be. They used to say, we were packed like sardines—that is, small, cheap, tightly packed. He was not a sardine in the cannery—no, he was one measly, fat gray sardine in a large hollow tin, dark and full of echoes.

One night, he heard a noise among the noises, a singular clank among the many tiny mouse/rat jangles. Ignore it, must be nothing, making it up, hearing things. Imagining. Stars. Make that sound. He sang to himself, and it went away. Didn't hear it again. Only the dripping of time.

He went back out and out into the days of the week as he'd always done, against the onslaught of the wonderful story that wasn't, against death and everybody, and the perpetual unanswerable question: Where you from? Something was always lost.

He muttered this to himself, smiled, ducked, and pried his way into the cannery, downed the light, and walked as if through the salt cod black sea—

A falling shoosh, and suddenly he was surrounded by something like shantung, first word came to his mind. Don't know why, but whatever the fabric, it draped on him with a stultifying gauze weight, he couldn't move, and when he tried, he only made it worse.

He bellowed.

"You sound like a sea cow. Relax." A woman's voice. She stepped out. "I caught ya, didn't I? Netted ya just like they used to in the old days out there on the high seas."

He grunted.

"Didn't I, didn't I ..." She tittered and paced, did a little gotcha-shuffle, and her rag of robes spun around her in a twirling fanfare. "Yes, I did."

The hours revealed her to be Anty, or maybe Aunty, she didn't spell it. Another drifter, but with a bit of a ... weird streak. He didn't know. She had as much gray hair on her head as he did on his face; together, they'd be a full gray ball of head and face.

"You're such a catch," she said like he was a young doctor she'd lassoed into marriage.

After some time, his blood pressure came back down, he could think again, talk.

"Water ..." he croaked. "Water ..."

"Oh, you big baby, I'm not going to starve you. I ain't gonna let you waste away."

And she didn't. She fed him nice. Hot coffee from somewhere, tasty little victuals for the setting, chips, cured meat. But she also didn't let him go. She stayed chatty. In time, everything changes, and although they were still strangers with an element of danger, they became something else.

Anty told him her story, the glossed-over version that hid the deep and terrible lows—they weren't that close yet—but spun them into an honest, vulnerable pitch with a pinch of sass, you know what I mean.

Brother Adam began to talk too beneath the net. It was like he was talking through a darkened web, because he was, but for some reason, surprising to him, this was comforting, and indeed even inspired a certain loquacity that hadn't peeked out of him in years and years of the downtrodden. Captivity, in fact, seemed to suit him, giving way to a fishy domesticity that eventually forced them to confront each other.

"What are we doing?!"

"Why did you trap me?"

"Why didn't you put up more of a fight?"

"Are you crazy?"

"Are you crazy?"

Indeed, love, or one of its derivatives, had taken root. And speaking of root, she got under the net there with him. In other words, they fucked like old people, which is to say they knew what they were doing, which is to say they also didn't want to hurt themselves. The fishery took on another fishy smell. They complimented each other.

Time passed in little crunk components. Little fits and starts. Dissolved, bubbled back up to float, pool, eddy, rage forward with a king tide, and pull way back to the ocean's edge.

Spring came, and they didn't hate each other. Then, strangest of strangest, she began to show.

"What's that?"

"My bump."

"Your bump. You bump like that? You been swallowing whole bowling balls?"

"I think I'm bumping a baby."

"Thought you mega-paused and all that."

"Me too. Guess not."

"Huh. Don't know what I think about that."

"Me neither."

And so they did their best not to think about it at all. But, as babies do, that belly interjected itself into about everything. It had its way. Emergent. Like everybody's already been born, and I want to do it too.

"Will I have a gray-haired baby?" she thought. "An old soul? As they say …" She prepared. She didn't know who "they" were, but knew they did indeed say it.

He thought about the old days, thought back as far as he could, but couldn't get back to babydom, that misty memory field fallow as any blackness. What would they do?

The problem was that time ate itself, and before either of them had a bead on perpetuity, it came out in a rush of water. The baby. The boy. A whole lot of loving to keep my baby happy, true true, and they called him Sardine because of his silvery skin, puckered mouth, and he was so darn small, compact. How it takes a whole lot of kissing and hugging. A whole lot of decision-making.

And they decided, or it was decided for them because the weather was getting warmer, earlier, and it became harder to be themselves with their squatting frugality in a swelling town of tourists, and so they decided to set their baby free, because all babies, as everybody knows, want to be free and so they set Sardine into the ocean to be free, feed everybody with his flesh, ubiquitous, breed and make merry. Throw your young body against the waves and come up clean, son, once uncountable volumes, come back, quicksilver, come back, torn by the spirits swimming through our world. In a word: hope.

"Into the Mist" by Don Peterson

SPRING TIDE

Richard Foerster

York, Maine

Ten eel-necked cormorants, journeying
somewhere north, rest on the rocks' last knuckle

that points from this cove out toward the indefinable
line. There a beacon, bleared by thin fog,

searches the evening's depths beyond Boon Island.
The sea lies flat as rippled slate.

One could think of walking out on it,
except that the imperceptible heaving

cracks into whiteness at the cormorants' feet.
Suddenly I am caught up in the hush

of ritual. The birds splay their ancient wings
to the tentative air, hold them, poised

and priestly, as if inviting a necessary prayer.
There's such trembling in this waiting

for a sign. But the moment passes, and the birds
bend their awkward bills to preening.

The light grows dim. The wheel-eyed beacon stares
and turns. What could I recite if now, on the verge

of losing sight of them and wanting
home, they'd assume their singular grace and fly?

SEA GLASS

Michelle Choiniere

along the jagged edges
of the coastline I love
lay pieces of mysteries
left to be told

hundreds of people
scour the wreckage
looking for something
worth being sold

but I look out of wonder
at the memories caught
in the graveyard of stories
here on these shores

to find what I'm missing
or learn from the past
to see what it offers and
fling open its doors

the pebbles that look so
uniform and round
hold the key to a story
yet to be found

a memory of a sailor
a jar of preserves
or the tale of a ship
sunk to the ground

I gather them up
and carry them home
they set in my window
catching the light

just like the lighthouse
from which they came
lost long ago on
one stormy night

BLUE SHARK

Rick Doyle

The sun stood burning at zenith.
But for a couple of smallish cod
and a meager pack of dogfish
no one had been catching anything
for hours, so we ventured farther out
on the salt-heaped desert wilderness,
we went running after the horizon,
after the molten bead of gold
where sun had soldered sea and
sky together early. It got late, malaise set in.
The first mate pitched a fit,
flinging buckets of chum out
onto the surging wake, bringing
down snow-white, hungry gulls
and gaffing the sharks that came to beg.
Unheralded, then, or heralded only
by the lesser blue sharks that begged
and were lifted by their gaping gills,
or by a seasonal curdling of the sky,
this cobalt god, this quarter-ton cobalt maul
rolled to bone-white under the hull and away.
Waves broke around us, we were far from shore.
Back on land? The seething silver
of the little birch leaves, tormented
near dusk by a freshening breeze, shivering
behind the weathered gazebo. Echo. Mere echo.
Help us, o father! Old Father Neptune! Help us
to hear the empty salt waves seething in the sun.

COASTAL TEMPEST

Marjorie Arnett

A dead calm afternoon,
silence overflows with desire.
A tiny leaf quivers, then brushes
another warning of a breeze
that conjures a storm.

Clouds roll in, pile up like sea foam
building on a shore. Air darkens,
threatening clouds form an armada
advancing on a plane of air.

As if poured from buckets, water
drenches, ripping leaves off trees.
Jags of lightning sage a strange
wild unholy light and the world
kneels down in disbelief.

The deluge continues then trails off.
Low riding afternoon sun filters
onto land promising pale moon
fragments to come.

ENTANGLED

Ret Talbot

Sun slanted through scraggly evergreens, wretched and gnarled by winter storms slamming the island's weather side. Stiff, salt-soaked wind lashed from an expanse as large as any person's dreams or fears. Krill saw it on the granite. It was not clear, but knowing it was a shark, he imagined it.

It was beautiful.

"Wipitamekw," Nick's father said in that measured way Native people his age speak. "Multi-toothed one."

Nick checked his phone for a signal. Jonathon leaned in. He looked a little too enthusiastic about the 4,000-year-old petroglyph. He was a pleaser. Krill suspected the scientists were thinking about an actual shark out in the Atlantic—about catching and tagging it with a satellite tag. They were thinking about science, what they'd learn—what would be revealed. What could be known.

The first time he'd seen the petroglyph, Krill knew he needed this moment in his book. It could've been the set-up for a joke: a fifty-something Caucasian shark biologist, a young Native scientist, and an elder walk into a bar. But this wasn't a joke. This was important. It all came down to this—these men, this island, and a shark.

"There are many ways of knowing a thing," Nick's father said. "There are the old ways, which tell us who we are, but there is also other knowledge— knowledge that may be useful to you." He looked at Jonathan and his son. "But it is our knowledge to share."

The *Jenny Ann*'s hull slammed against the dark ocean. Barry, a lobsterman of Native descent like most of the men on the island, was at the helm. Cliff, also Native, was at the stern with Jonathan and Nick. The fishing rods were stowed. The remaining chum was dumped. The scientists' instruments remained in their Pelican cases, stowed in the small cabin. Krill maintained his distance, his journalistic objectivity.

Cliff spotted a seal. "We need blubber."

Jonathan knew that wasn't true—he'd hooked big sharks on tuna and mackerel, but he agreed that blubber would help, especially for a big shark. An old shark. Jonathan held a federal permit to harvest tissue from marine mammals for scientific use, but his permit didn't allow him to hunt them.

"We need a dead whale," Jonathan said.

Jonathan, Nick, and Krill walked up the hill to Nick's father's house. They were tired after a long day at sea. Jonathan checked his email. A colleague had forwarded a Coast Guard report—a navigational hazard near their location. A dead whale was drifting several miles upwind of the island. If there was a big shark, it would feed on that whale. Nick ran down to the village and found Cliff at Barry's house playing dominoes with tiles made out of whale bone.

Barry and Cliff agreed to look for the whale at dawn.

The day had dawned snotty. An ugly bank of unruly clouds hunched on the horizon. Squalls circled. Barry was steady, feet shoulder-width apart, hands on the wheel. The wipers sluiced sheets of rain from the windscreen.

Barry consulted his charts and the unwritten knowledge in every fisherman's head. They searched all day.

"It's too good to be true," Jonathan said, huddled in the wheelhouse with the others.

Barry turned to face them and shook his head. He didn't have to say it.

They all silently agreed.

The research trip was over. There was no shark, even though big sharks appeared here annually at this time, according to the old stories. According to the petroglyph. Nick told Jonathan about it when he first interned with him. That was before Jonathan became his PhD adviser. Jonathan was skeptical. He'd have heard of this place. Science would know about a reliable aggregation site for big sharks. Nick became skeptical too, but they were at Bigelow for a conference, so they were practically already there. It was the right time of year, and the federal authorities had suspended the lobster season. Getting a boat wouldn't be hard.

But they'd failed, and they were packing their gear. Nick's father was in the next room watching a show about polar bears with the volume too loud. Krill was staring at his laptop, panicked. Except for the Inuit hunter on the television, the mood was somber.

Peggy Smith knocked. She was the schoolteacher at the one-room schoolhouse that wasn't one room but operated as such. Peggy was from away, but she'd taught at the school for sixteen years. Krill met her during his scouting trip for the project. He knew immediately she needed to be in his narrative. As a teacher and as one of a handful of white people living on the island, she symbolized one way of knowing. One type of knowledge.

"The whale washed up on Put'p Rock," Peggy said. Her eyes moved from Krill to the others, then back to Krill. "This means you'll stay?"

As much as Krill worked to maintain distance and objectivity regarding the others, he'd failed with Peggy. He'd gone to her house after getting back from their futile search for the whale. He told her they were leaving. She was upset.

"How do you know the whale washed up on Put'p Rock?" Nick asked.

"Tina from WGM," she said. "They're coming tomorrow because NMFS can't get people out right away."

Nick frowned. Peggy's students had studied critically endangered North Atlantic right whales. A woman from Whale Guardians of Maine, a non-profit group dedicated to whale response and education, came to speak. It had pissed off the islanders. Lobstering was one of the few jobs. It was no secret that WGM wanted the fishery closed.

WGM, with a coalition of powerful environmental and animal welfare groups, argued the lobster fishery—or more specifically, the vertical lines connecting traps to buoys—posed an unacceptable level of entanglement risk. A U.S. district court agreed, ruling that, in authorizing the lobster fishery, federal fisheries managers failed to comply with the Endangered Species Act. Lobstermen worried this could be the last nail, even though there was no conclusive evidence that a right whale had ever been entangled in Maine gear.

Jonathan sympathized. He'd butted heads with WGM. The whale folks were too biased for his scientific mind—how they named the whales and were fanatical about them. The last time he'd tried to harvest tissue from a dead whale, WGM got involved. When he arrived at the beach, WGM volunteers had cordoned it off and anchored the carcass to a guardrail so it wouldn't refloat at high tide. A young volunteer told Jonathan they were "acting under a federal standing agreement with NOAA" and had the "legal authority to prevent anyone from interfering with the carcass until a National Marine Fisheries-designated response team arrived."

Jonathan showed him his permit.

"So you can use her as bait?" The volunteer got in Jonathan's face. "The hell you are!"

A local reporter noticed the raised voices. Jonathan didn't like the optics, even if he was right. He walked away.

Suddenly, Nick's father was in the room. Nobody knew he'd been listening. "Put'p Rock is a sacred island belonging to the People," he said. "Just as the whale is a sacred animal."

They looked at Nick's father, but he said nothing else before returning to the television.

"What does that mean?" Krill asked.

"Dunno," Nick said. "Sometimes I think he just says stuff he thinks sounds right—like the old ways."

Nick brewed coffee before dawn. They'd stayed up late talking. Jonathan had made up his mind. The petroglyph was cool, and it was interesting meeting his student's father and seeing the island on which he'd grown up, but even if the big sharks once came here before heading offshore, he'd observed nothing to indicate they were here now. If this were an aggregation site, a tagged shark would've pinged here. He'd searched the literature and combed through the data. Nothing. Science was about using scarce resources judiciously, not pursuing unsubstantiated stories.

Yet he'd ultimately agreed to stay two more days. As the previous night seeped deeper toward dawn, Nick became contemplative about the whale on Put'p Rock. Put'p, in the language of the People, meant "whale." Was that a coincidence? The dead whale appearing just when they decided to leave?

"Of course, it was," Jonathan thought. "Correlation is not causation." He agreed to go to Put'p Rock at first light, harvest whale blubber, and make one final attempt to find the shark.

Jonathan was, after all, a pleaser.

It was calm when they rounded Sekewa't Head, the place with the shark petroglyph. Barry pointed *Jenny Ann*'s bow north. It'd blown hard overnight. The sky was cloudless. Put'p Rock appeared as a smudge that gained definition until it became a fir-covered island for most of its length before ending in a barren, rocky prow.

Barry pointed to smoke.

"I thought it was uninhabited," Krill said.

"It is. That looks like a campfire."

They rounded the prow and came to a small, steep cobble beach. Above where the twenty-foot tide piled flotsam, there was a tent bright yellow against dark firs. Beside the fire was a figure who stood when the *Jenny Ann* appeared. Barry backed the engine down. All they heard was the slap of water against the hull. The figure lifted binoculars. Barry did the same.

"Looks like a woman," Barry said. "She's wearing a WGM sweatshirt."

"How'd she get here already?" Nick asked.

"I'm guessing they came yesterday." Jonathan recalled the horrible sea state. "She must have wanted to get here."

"I don't see a boat," Krill said.

"They probably anchored on the other side," Barry answered, seeing the woman was now waving her hands over her head. "We should check it out. Nick, go with Cliff."

Cliff brought the dinghy alongside.

Krill scanned the coast with the binoculars. "Where's the whale?"

"It should've beached here," Barry said. "But who knows with that wind."

Cliff started the dinghy's outboard. Nick settled into the bow. The dinghy cut a frothed curve toward the beach. When shallow enough, Nick went over the side, the bow line in his hand. The woman approached. From the *Jenny Ann*, they heard the dinghy's hull scrape on the cobbles, but they couldn't hear the conversation.

Eventually, Nick got back into the boat. The woman returned to the fire.

Back aboard the *Jenny Ann*, Nick said, "The whale disappeared overnight."

"Disappeared?" Krill asked.

"Likely during the high tide," Barry said. "Full moon."

"I thought they anchored carcasses," Jonathan said.

"Dunno," Nick replied. "I guess she didn't. Says she was dropped off with another guy yesterday. His leg got wrecked between the dinghy and the beach when landing, so they took him back. Tina stayed."

"Whale hugger," Barry said, shaking his head.

"Anyways," Nick said, "I told her we'd circle the island. Look for the whale. I offered to give her a ride back. She's going to pack up and be ready when we return."

"Great," Barry said. He didn't mean it.

They circumnavigated Put'p Rock but didn't see the whale. Barry thought he knew where it had drifted, but it was getting late, and the USCG was issuing another storm warning.

Jonathan apologized to Nick. "We tried," he said. "It seems like the gods are against us."

Tina was waiting, her drybag packed. Once she was aboard, Barry set a course to the island.

Krill leaned against the wheelhouse beside Tina, who smelled of wood smoke. Put'p Rock got smaller in the wake. Barry hadn't said a word to her, and she'd not thanked him. Cliff was with Barry at the helm. Jonathan and Nick were below organizing their gear.

"They say Put'p Rock is sacred to the People," Krill said.

Tina looked at the two Native men at the helm of the *Jenny Ann*. "It seems like *these people* have lost their way."

"That's harsh."

She scowled. "They make a living at the expense of one of the greatest animals ever to inhabit this planet. It's sickening."

"The People used to hunt whales," Krill countered.

"That's different," she said, hesitating. "Things were in balance then. We don't know balance anymore." Put'p Rock disappeared into the sea. "At least I know right from wrong."

Krill thought about that—about what we know and how we know it.

That evening, Jonathan and Nick hitched a ride with a Maine Department of Marine Resources pilot who'd flown out to look for the whale. They offered Tina the fourth seat on the plane, but she was waiting for WGM volunteers to come out with a boat to search for the whale. Tina would stay with Peggy. Krill left with the scientists.

Krill wondered why Tina seemed so keen on finding the whale. Either it'd beach somewhere else, or it'd be eaten by sharks and disappear forever.

Krill didn't learn the truth until he returned to the island for Nick's father's funeral. He hadn't spoken to Peggy. Having given up on the book, he instead wrote a series of articles about Nick's career as a promising young shark biologist who incorporated traditional ecological knowledge into his research. Nick had returned to his father's stories about big sharks appearing at the island each autumn. It was a new way of analyzing their migrations in a timescale far greater than science had previously considered. The resulting systems-level understanding triggered a paradigm shift in how scientists thought about the Atlantic Meridional Overturning Circulation. That led to many discoveries, including, much to Jonathan's chagrin, the mating grounds of the big sharks.

Back on the island, Krill picked up easily with Peggy, though no longer romantically. On the morning of his departure, he asked Peggy to walk up Sekewa't Head with him so he could see the shark petroglyph again. When the sun hit it, the shark was more clearly defined than he remembered.

"You remember when Tina stayed with me?" Peggy asked out of the blue.

"Yes."

"She showed me pictures of the whale she had on her phone."

"I didn't know she had pictures."

"She did," Peggy said, looking out over the ocean. Her voice quivered. "There were purple markings on the rope entangling the whale."

Krill knew what that meant. By law, Maine lobster gear was marked with purple. "I never heard that," he said. "I mean, when they reopened the fishery with the new regulations, even the federal judge said there's no irrefutable evidence of a right whale entangled in Maine gear."

Peggy looked in the direction of Put'p Rock with tears in her eyes. He took her hand.

"I deleted the pictures while Tina slept."

Peggy cried openly now.

"They must've found the whale, though?" Krill asked, confused.

"I told Barry about the photos." Her body wracked with sobs. She put her hand on the rock above the petroglyph to steady herself. Her chest heaved. Snot ran from her nostrils. "He and Cliff," she stammered. "Barry and Cliff went out that night, found her, and blew her up."

SEA SWIM

Erin Covey-Smith

Becoming horizon, and amniotic
held by cold joy and forever
neck-deep in a bath of silky silence
cupped and capped by vastness—
sea, sky, and deliverance
from bearing to borne.

WINDEYES

Patricia Smith Ranzoni

Cape Rosier. Land's end.
Numbing cold (goes without
saying). I'll be damned
if these winds (*orchestral*)
are not having their way
with the ocean. Waves surging
back and *back* (not *in*)
(*against the tide I mean*).
Never seen the likes of it, you?
This tidal pool shaking
under windflaws, one thing,
but waves rolling out
instead of forward what do you
make of it? As if, always there
for the shore, the sea today
is being loved in return.

Windeyes: Old Norse for "windows," before glass.

"Seen-Unseen" by Lisa Tyson Ennis

SKIM ICE

Gro Flatebo

Six degrees at 7 a.m. and a light mist rises from the river. Sunrise, peeking through low clouds over Lanes Island, fills my house with rose light. The forested shoreline is a palette of gray, dark green, and brown, and the slate-colored water is still, with no ripples. I feel the steadfastness of the river and the sea on these cold, cold mornings and treasure them because, as our climate changes, they are becoming rarer.

I've lived near the mouth of the Royal River in Yarmouth, Maine, for twenty years. When we first built our house, our three children were home, and I didn't have a room to work and write in until they left home. Instead, I sat in a little window seat facing the river, watching its daily and seasonal changes.

The tidal river empties into Casco Bay, flowing both ways depending on the tide. Broad expanses of mudflats emerge on either side of a narrow channel twice a day. The river is alive with lobstermen, aquaculture workers, paddlers, sport anglers, and pleasure boaters. In the spring and fall, boat traffic is light, and I hear the deep thrum of diesel engines from lobster and work boats. In the summer, the sound from scads of pleasure boats shifts to whiny outboard motors, stereo systems playing pop and country music, and the thud of wakes smashing the shoreline.

Winter here is my favorite season, because then the river is mine—no oak or maple leaves to block my view and no noise. Wildlife—eagles, coyotes, deer, wild turkeys—comes down to the shore, where the temperatures are milder and there is less snow and more food. A few working boats remain after the fall—mostly lobster boats converted to draggers. With the storms, high winds, and shockingly cold water, it's a hard way to make a living.

Where I live, people have shaped the river for hundreds of years, but these changes are rarely permanent. Piles of clam and oyster shells dot the shore, evidence of Wabanaki summer campsites and the rich bounty the estuary had to offer. The Native Americans were upset about the pollutants and the damage to the river after Europeans arrived in the mid-1600s and set up sawmills. This was but one of several factors that fomented their attacks on the settlers.

In the 1700s, a dam upriver generated hydropower for a shoe factory, tannery, sawmill, and other industries. A second dam downriver was built in the late 1800s to power a textile mill, and later provide electricity. Between the two dams, a large paper and pulp mill straddled the river from the early 1900s to the 1960s. After world pulp markets collapsed, the mill was demolished, partially obstructing the river channel with concrete blocks and brick debris. Industries have long left the river. Any toxic pollutants in the sediments have been scoured out by countless nor'easters and hurricanes. Now, the lower river hosts three marinas and boatyards. The town took over the woodyard and paper mill property, which have been converted to a park.

I expect more changes on the river as Yarmouth and the U.S. Army Corps of Engineers prepare to remove the two dams and clear a channel of debris to allow migratory fish to pass—alewives, blueback herring, and American shad. One dam has been in place for over 300 years, the other over a hundred. Removing the dams will open up spawning sites and carry nutrients upstream to the headwaters. However, the proposal relies heavily on federal funds, so it may have to wait a few more years.

A wharf was built on our property in the 1800s. I call it a wharf, but now it's just a pile of rocks. Originally, it had three sheds to store bricks, hay, lumber, and apples before shipping to Boston by sloop. Winter ice has nearly scraped the wharf flat, sliding over the rocks and skimming off anything in its path. Today, only the rocks that formed the wharf's base and a little log cribwork hold it together. What's left is slippery and covered in kelp and algae, so we use an aluminum dock to launch our kayaks. This dock is pulled out each September, before the fall storms hit.

When the clear January nights were colder, the river would freeze hard, covering the expansive mudflats with up to two feet of ice. Blown smooth by arctic winds, the sherbet-green slab would rise and fall nine to twelve feet twice each day, cracking, shifting, then solidifying. When the heaving became too much, the ice crumpled onto the shore, like a stack of picnic napkins blown into a pile.

Back then, an ice-free pool often formed in front of my house, staying open from some anomaly of the currents. It attracted overwintering ducks, so eagles perched in our oaks to watch them feed. The ducks—scoters, eiders, and buffleheads—always clung together as a flock, careful not to stray too far. First a dozen, then none. Bloop, bloop, bloop, they'd dive down. One … two … bloop, bloop, bloop, they'd pop up. Where you once saw three, there'd be five, then nine. As they swam in the river, long V-shaped wakes spilled out behind, tracing their moves. When the tide went out, the ducks would work the shallows, afloat with heads down, looking like round river stones until they lifted their heads to breathe.

When the ice was thick each winter, coyotes paced back and forth on the opposite riverbank. Occasionally, they'd dart across, but the ice in the channel wasn't always solid. So they'd warily test the slush to see if it held. More often than not, they'd turn back to the shore. There were more coyotes across the river than I could see. I walked outside one night and heard a pack of at least half a dozen yelping. The adults were teaching the pups how to howl. It was haunting.

My neighbor, who lived on the river until she was ninety-six, told me that the ice always broke up by President's Day, in February. Her prediction was rooted in nearly a century of experience. The breakup was dramatic. Large sheets of ice moved quickly in and out of the river with the tides. The thick ice chunks could be up to forty feet long and submerge the channel buoys as they passed over them. Some would get stranded on my pile of rocks and perch, off-balance, over the tide cycle. Groups of ducks roosted on large ice blocks before drifting downstream. Hours later, the same ducks would ride upstream on the same block of ice with the incoming tide.

In the 1940s, my neighbor's uncle and a friend drowned on the river shortly after ice-out. He and his girlfriend got caught after sunset on Lanes

Island and tried to row back on a moonless night. They must have hit a chunk of ice drifting out of the river, capsizing their skiff and drowning in the icy waters. My neighbor had to identify their bodies. The woman wore red-striped mittens, and the color had bled onto her hands. She told me the girlfriend's hands were covered in bright red stripes.

In the winter of 2009, I hated the river ice. My sons, seventeen and fifteen, desperately wanted to skate on the river. We'd skated on the ocean once before, a magical day on an unsheltered reach where the windswept ice was glass and there were few underlying currents. We'd explored the frozen bubbles under the surface and let the wind gusts push us across the ice. The ricochet sound of ice cracking beneath us made us shiver. But the river channel near our house has strong, unseen currents that work the water downstream. The Cousins River joins in just before meeting Casco Bay, creating more underwater flow. These currents keep water moving and the ice from solidifying in the channel and other spots. It would carry my sons under if they fell through. I fought with my boys for an entire weekend, forbidding them to go. It was hard to argue that the ice and channel were dangerous when they saw thick ice blocks pushed up on the shoreline. All I could think about was the red-striped mittens.

The next weekend, my sons and two friends snuck out to skate on their own. They survived. It was better that I didn't know they were out there.

Today, the effects people have on the river are more insidious and may be permanent. Recent winters are logging in as some of the warmest on record. Average temperatures have risen nearly four degrees Fahrenheit since the 1980s, with winters changing faster than other seasons. January nights are no longer cold enough for the river to freeze. Most years, our winters aren't really winters. The ducks are scattered along the shoreline rather than concentrated in the pool off our rocks.

These days, there is little ice, so no ice-out. Skim ice and blocks still form in the upper harbor and ride out on the tides, but it's not like before. The skim ice is too thin for the ducks to roost on, and is easily broken up by the buoys. I only know it's there by its rough texture, which doesn't reflect the sky.

If I sound nostalgic, I am. I love the solitude of the frozen river and the winter rhythms. I never expected to see such a dramatic and tangible shift in the climate within just two decades. Unlike the dams, these warming changes are nearly impossible to reverse. I feel powerless and vulnerable because there is no consistent political will to take action.

I'm parochial in focusing on my backyard, but aren't all politics local? These are changes I see and feel. They're amplified in the Gulf of Maine, which since the 1980s has warmed three times as much as the oceans.

In 2025, for the first time in over a decade, the river froze solid—the pool off our wharf opened, and the ducks gathered. I watched them on the river whenever I could. The ice wasn't two feet thick, but it was solid. I was comforted to see it again, but knew it was an aberration, teasing me to believe that cold winters were back. The ice broke up in early February, three weeks earlier than my neighbor's prediction.

My sons now have children of their own. My grandchildren may never see the ducks gather off our shore, the coyotes trying to cross the channel, or two-foot slabs of ice floating back and forth on the tide. The sounds of ice cracking and thundering as it breaks up may only be preserved in the stories I tell them. My sons won't have to argue with them about skating on the river because the river may never ice over again.

KAPLAN'S COASTAL BLUES

Jay Franzel

Seeking a town where trains rack, the line ends
and hill roads bend to the sea, I reached a lonely place.
Here, where ships dock, the sea breathes,
and icy bay creaks in white harbor
I turned wool to winter and walked past the siding
beside tall conifers, their boughs heavy with snow
that glowed under moonlight, steel glinting
silence shuddering with each sudden coupling
metal echoes shaking down snow.
I was lost, it was cold, everything deepening.

VINALHAVEN

Marianne Stratton

No one is awake, we tiptoe from the house,
filled with our sisters, side by side in rooms like bony fish
down the salt dew lawn, towels in hand,
past the boat house smelling of linseed,
stony cove dressed in rockweed and bladderwrack, slick and robust
two days have passed since the docking and still the island
keeps us bridal veiled and shrouded, a legendary Avalon
half-finished Zion, clouded and salt drenched

even the sky has forgotten who she is

Imogen dives into the trusting arms of the saline bay
I take the aluminum ladder, one step, two and release
fall into icy August black water that may well be the sky
her with practiced strokes, muscle memory of lifeguard
years and daughter days, me, I dive and emerge
once, twice and manifest an ancient tail of sorts

the house silhouettes in gauzy obscura and we swim

These our numbered years, quartz crystal bodies absorbing
each other's losses until that too fails, inevitability is still a god
when only Imogen remains we will come for her at daybreak
a sea of purple through the mist, even then.
I float in her wake at the opaque edge of the dream morning
ruffled winged kelp, *alaria esculenta,* circles my legs like cats
sentient and recording our wordless oaths by the floating dock
you will not be alone for long

only the footprint of the house remains visible

"Jasper Beach" by Leslie Dale Bowman

LIGHTHOUSES IN THE SKY

Nomar Slevik

I have been enchanted by small-town Maine my entire life. Living in and traveling to these villages, each with its unique charm, history, and quiet mysteries, is a privilege. But sometimes, that enchantment takes a little time.

My family and I moved from Fort Kent to the small coastal village of Northeast Harbor in 1987, and everything was different. We were a long way from home, I missed my friends, and the area had yet to work its magic on me. I was about to start fourth grade in a school where I didn't know a soul, and that first year was rough; I felt isolated. As the chubby new kid, I had my fair share of bullies, but it was the loneliness that got to me. I was introverted, but after a while, I did manage to make a few good friends. Without even realizing it, the little coastal town snuck its way into my northern Maine heart.

By the summer of 1989, I was eleven going on eighteen, and spending a lot of time at my best friend's house. He lived in Somesville, and we played video games, blasted nothing but hip-hop, and watched a whole bunch of horror movies. I was into the paranormal then too, but my friends weren't all that interested, so I mostly kept it to myself. My mom shared my fascination, and she'd tell me ghost stories, ones she'd experienced. My dad was a skeptic, but never dismissed my curiosity. In fact, he was the one who brought something curious to my attention.

On the early evening of July 27, my friend's mother dropped me off after I'd spent the afternoon at his house. When I walked inside, my father was in his favorite chair reading *The Bar Harbor Times*. He pointed out a report, but at my age, I couldn't imagine a newspaper containing anything that would grab my attention. Then, I saw it, the three-letter acronym that would forever consume my curiosity: "UFO."

Here's an excerpt of the report:

> "Two pilots flying over Blue Hill Bay claimed to have seen a
> UFO in the vicinity of Swan's Island. 'I've got 4,500 hours
> of flying time as a commercial pilot, and I've never seen any-
> thing like this during the day,' said Randy Rhodes, who was
> flying with a lawyer friend, Bill Reiff. They described it as a
> metallic, oblong-shaped disk that moved extremely quickly
> in one direction, stopped, then moved again."

The encounter instantly gripped me. I carefully stored the newspaper away; it may have been the first otherworldly artifact I ever tried to archive. Regrettably, through several moves in my adult life, I lost it. But the fascination, the sheer wonder of that report, has never left me.

That sighting was just one of the many strange and compelling stories tied to the Maine coast. From mysterious lights to strange entities, the coastline holds more than its share of the unexplained. Here, I'll share more of these encounters, stories that have stayed with me over the years.

The Surry Light Bulb

A little over twenty-seven miles northwest of Mount Desert Island, where wild cranberries grow and scattered boulders mark the roads, lies the town of Surry. The center of this hamlet sits at the knifepoint's end of Patten Bay and is close enough to MDI to get out and enjoy Acadia National Park. You can then escape back to the calm, avoiding the island's seasonal chaos. But Surry isn't just a place to retreat. With its network of hiking trails and winding river shores, it offers plenty of outdoor adventures without the crowds of Bar Harbor. And in the summer of 1979, two locals stumbled into something they couldn't explain.

Around 10 p.m., Mrs. Dickinson sat inside her enclosed porch, enjoying her view of Patten Bay. She was used to seeing the lights of small-engine aircraft approach the Hancock County-Bar Harbor Airport, and tonight seemed no different. Just then, a friend arrived, parked his car, and stepped onto the porch to join her. Before he said a word, something outside, just beyond the porch, caught his eye, and he gasped.

Dickinson turned to face him, then followed his gesture to the window and saw what had startled him. It was a bizarre object, and she watched as it glided just feet from the house. "Any closer, it would have scraped the paint," she later recalled. She had seen strange lights in the sky before but nothing like this. It was a small, translucent vessel that resembled a light bulb. "Just big enough for one occupant," she observed, "and shaped like an antique Mazda Edison Electric light bulb. I know. I have a couple."

Inside ... they saw an occupant.

It was a small creature, about three feet tall, with an oblong head described as having "the layered, bandaged look" of a wasp's nest. The creature sat on a pale blue box, its right hand extended toward a control panel. It had large, black eyes but no visible mouth, nose, or ears. Its left arm "sort of hung at its side, and its feet hardly touched the floor."

As the craft slowly glided past them, the creature mechanically turned its head and locked eyes with Dickinson. The movement was unnatural—"a porcelain doll, swivel-headed," she later described. Before she could even process the sight, the craft vanished. Not knowing what else to do, the pair retreated to the living room to discuss what had happened. She thought it could have been a "scout craft" from a larger UFO that loomed somewhere above them. As they continued talking, the craft reappeared by her neighbor's home and then vanished once more.

Come morning, they searched the area but found nothing unusual. They even wandered onto the property next door to take a look. When the neighbor stepped outside and asked what they were doing, they told them about the incident and asked if they had seen anything. They hadn't, but looked concerned. Dickinson decided not to mention the UFO so haphazardly after that.

"I knew my world would never again be the same," she later said. "I had seen a number of lovely spacecrafts, but as long as they were way up in the sky, they did not concern me. This, however, was another matter."

In time, Dickinson found others who had also seen the craft, but were unwilling to publicly share their sightings. The scrutiny concerned them, which comes with the unexplained.

The strange visitor to Surry may have vanished, but I imagine for those who saw it, the memory lingered for quite some time.

The Hooded Entities of Bar Harbor

Local UFO researcher Shirley Fickett investigated a strange case out of Bar Harbor that took place two months before Dickinson's sighting. On a June evening, at around 10 p.m., a sixteen-year-old boy named Ralph had just left his girlfriend's house. As he made his way along the sidewalk, he saw a small creature ahead of him. He thought it could have been a raccoon or maybe a small dog. But something felt ... off. Concerned, he stepped onto the road to avoid it. The moment he did, the creature vanished from his thoughts. The usual nighttime sounds faded, and more unsettling, there were no cars on the road. Strange for Bar Harbor in the summer when the streets are typically packed with tourists, even late at night. But now? It was silent.

Ralph unknowingly drifted toward the center of the road. He stood there confused when suddenly, the ground was flooded with a brilliant white light. Fickett later wrote, "As the light shone around him on the ground, he seemed at a loss for words in describing how the buildings around him looked. It was like there was a revolving light above, as you see in dance halls, displaying various colors on the buildings—red, blue, etc."

The next moment, Ralph's perspective inexplicably changed; he was no longer on the ground but up in the air, looking down at the road. Then, just as suddenly, he was lying on a table. Shadowy figures moved around him, and panic set in.

Then, just as suddenly as it had begun, it was over. He was back on the road and in a mid-sprint! As he looked over his shoulder, the shadowy figures were gliding toward him. Ahead, his house came into view. He could see the front door; his only goal was to get inside. Suddenly, the figures called out to him. Fickett wrote, "[They were] calling for him to come back. That they wouldn't harm him."

He reached the door, threw it open, and ran inside. As he slammed and locked it, he heard from the other side, "We'll be back!" He turned around, and in the entryway sat his two younger sisters, staring at him. The older of the two, only four years old, looked up at him and asked, "Who just said they'd be back?"

He didn't answer. He didn't know how to. It didn't even strike him as odd that they were awake, sitting by the door. Instead, he ran upstairs to his parents' room, waking them to tell of his terrifying encounter. Before he could say anything, he saw their clock. It was much later than it should have been. It was after midnight; he'd lost almost two hours.

While telling his parents about the encounter, the shadowy figures came into focus for him. He remembered that there were three of them, all cloaked and hooded in silver fabric. He couldn't recall any facial features, only a black void where their faces should have been.

Ralph never fully understood what happened to him that night, and it remains unknown if the cloaked figures returned.

It Wasn't a Cruise Ship

Before I met my best friend, I spent my preteen nights huddled around my boombox, listening to Ice-T spin tales of gangster life on the streets of Los Angeles—quite the contrast, I know. The hypnotic basslines, crafted by producer Afrika Islam, transported my young mind to another world. By seventeen, a lot of us spent most of our early evenings after school cruising the streets of Bar Harbor, looking as cool as Ice-T, I imagined. In reality, we were just driving around the same four roads, doing what we called "laps." With no cell phones, we communicated via CB radio. We smoked cigarettes and weed, and avoided the cops. The Iceman would have been proud.

One night in February 1994, my friend and I noticed some odd lights floating down the Mount Desert Narrows, heading toward the pier. We tracked them as we drove along West Street, but with businesses blocking our view, my friend suggested we go to Grant Park near the shore path. I turned onto Main Street and passed Geddy's on the right, then Sherman's Book Shop and Ben & Bill's on the left. As we neared Cool As A Moose, I flicked on my blinker and turned down Albert Meadow. Pulling into the lot, the lights on the water came into view. We stepped out and walked to the water's edge for a better look.

We stood there, marveling as the giant, silent "thing" floated past us. There were at least ten rows of white lights from top to bottom. There was no sound, left no wake—just moved slowly and steadily at around twenty miles per hour. We could only speculate. A cruise ship? Unlikely. It was winter. I suggested a UFO, but my friend shrugged and sighed. "Maybe," he said. We watched until it floated out of sight.

When I got home, I wrote down the entire experience, which I've since also lost. That year, UFO sightings were reported across the state, from Belfast to Sebago Lake, but none matched what we'd seen. About six months later, my dad handed me another newspaper article about a sighting.

I remember it clearly, a late Saturday morning. My dad casually mentioned an article in the Saturday edition of the *Bangor Daily News* about UFO sightings in Maine. My teenage angst morphed to childlike joy as I snagged the paper and ran back up to my room; I was eleven years old again.

I just about bowled over when the article started with an encounter from Southwest Harbor, a town less than thirty minutes from my incident months prior. I saved that article too, which has also been lost. The curse of a young person's disorganization and too many moves. (I swear I'm better at this now!)

Good news, I found it on Newspapers.com. The following is an excerpt from the September 24, 1994, article "UFO Network Collects Sightings of Alien Spacecraft":

> "Last January, during a power outage in Southwest Harbor, a couple woke up at 3 a.m. and witnessed a bright beam of light shining down on a patch of woods across a bay. Red, green, and blue lights were coming from the top of the beam, but clouds obscured their view further. There was no rational explanation for what they saw."

I remember asking my mom if she'd heard about the sighting since she worked in town at the time. She hadn't. However, a friend from high school told me about a sighting at their home in Southwest Harbor.

Eating breakfast on the balcony overlooking the harbor, he heard a splash and looked up to see a column of falling water. Overhead, he was stunned to see a silver ball hovering about a hundred feet above him. Then, in an instant, it shot off at incredible speed.

Around this time, a couple attending the College of the Atlantic in Bar Harbor encountered a bizarre entity on a dirt road. The pair were headed to a bonfire in the woods, a thing we did in the nineties (do kids still do that?). They were having trouble finding the turnoff and had just crested the top of a hill when they saw something strange in the road. It was pale, human-shaped, and "crab walking upside down across the road." Suddenly, it stood up and ran the rest of the way and into the woods. Terrified, they turned around, abandoning the bonfire.

WINDWARD SIDE

As strange as these encounters may seem, they are part of the fabric of life here along the Maine coast. From the quiet villages to the shifting tides, this weathered corner of the world is home to far more than meets the eye. I'm sure other areas of the world are similar, but this is the one that I know. It's where I was raised, side by side with the fog that rolls in off the ocean, as if it were a living, breathing cosmic entity. For those of us who call the coast home, the mystery is part of the magic.

SOURCES:

Anonymous. Ellsworth, Maine, August 1967. https://nuforc.org/webreports/reports/132/S132451.html.

Anonymous. "Pale Humanoid 'Crab-Walking' on Mount Desert Island, Maine Road." *Phantoms and Monsters,* July 17, 2022. https://www.phantomsandmonsters.com/2022/07/palehumanoid-crab-walking-on-mount. html?m=1.

Bechtel, Leland. "Reported UFO Sighting." *MUFON UFO Journal,* no. 259 (November 1989), 19–20.

Rosales, Albert S. *Humanoid Encounters 1975-1979: The Others Amongst Us.* CreateSpace, 2016.

Saltonstall, Polly. *The Bar Harbor Times*, July 27, 1989.

"Seated Occupant in Light-Bulb-Shape 1979 Maine CE-III." *CUFOS Associate Newsletter*, vol. 5, no. 2 (April–May 1984), 1–3.

"Town of Surry, Maine." https://www.townofsurrymaine.com/.

"UFO Network Collects Sightings of Alien Spacecrafts." *Bangor Daily News*, September 24, 1994.

THREE SOU'EASTERS AND A REDPOLL IN WINTER

Leslie Moore

—*After* High Tide *by Isabelle Maschal O'Donnell*

Each storm topples trees, breaches seawalls, leaves
a litter of sea wrack well beyond high tide marks.
Water floods parking lots, swamps restaurants,
casts aside picnic tables, park benches, boulders.
Waves sheer gangways from docks,
upheave planking from the harbor walk.

"Don't mess with water," a shipyard worker says
as he sweeps the sea out of a storage shed.

During one deluge, a redpoll lands on our porch railing,
side-steps to a dry spot under the eaves,
shakes his wet feathers and breathes.
His head is spiked red.

Climate crashes down on us, wave after wave.
Yet this little bird braves the gale.
Unabashed, he sings his tune, then wings
back into the storm.

SOME DAYS

Kara Douglas

We sit on your back porch in the late morning warmth.
You tell me your sternman went overboard.
You looked once and he was there, at the trap line.
You looked twice and he was gone.

I lean toward you, listening with every sinew.

You describe the feel of your knife slicing through rope,
the line going slack around his leg.
Best damn sternman you ever had.
He was also your son.
When you hauled him back aboard, he shook the water off
and set to pull the last few lines.

Despite our work-rough hands and steel hearts,
all these years later
we sit quietly on your porch and cry.

There is a moon rising now,
arched like a leaping fish in the great sky.
This truth you shared,
this mystery that is ours together
leaves us speechlessly whole.

A world hinges upon the breath you took just now.
And just now.
And just now.
The breath your son took when he surfaced
and the one you released when you pulled him to you and held on.

It hinges upon the monarch emerging from its chrysalis
the acorn that just fell,
the salamander's small gasp
the cloud that momentarily obscures the sun.

It hinges upon the story you tell
with tears in your eyes,
and it hinges upon the vast unknowing that may occupy our minds.

Somewhere between the deep sea of remembering
and the luminous sky of understanding,
we reside,
some days like a fish out of water,
some days reflecting the brilliance of a borrowed light,
some days like the generous emptiness of silence.

WELTERING

K. Stephens

A mass of warm air crossed the island long after the islanders had retired for the night. Water droplets conspired into a fine mist, roused from the last vestiges of snow, shrouding everything in sight.

Aaelene skimmed through the ground fog wrapped in a dark wool cloak. It was the opposite of finespun, a garment she'd made herself, generous and warm, with deep inner pockets. She kept to the ox trail in the center of the island, stopping every so often to stare up at the sky and get her bearings. Breath billowed from her hood.

The moon was bursting full, drenching the island. She could hear the tide already bucking for a fight. The spruce, pine, speckled alders, and birch that populated the island were in a party-line conversation. The snow had given them enough moisture to keep them healthy that winter. Inside their cambium, an ultra-low vibration spread from family to family. Each tree divined into the other with hundreds of intersecting limbs and twigs down to the fine root tips like a cat's cradle. Inside their root systems, she heard crackling fizzles. All were well-fed. None would wither and die this spring.

Aaelene strode through the highest points of the meadow, stopping to kneel and inspect a patch of new-growth dandelions. She plucked the basal rosettes and stuffed them inside her cloak pocket. The tender leaves would be sweet. She'd steep them tomorrow to ease the arthritic ache in Elray's nearly frostbitten hand and alleviate some of his bruises. She only thought of Elray for a moment out of habit. He was, by now, deep in sleep. She'd given him a powerful sedative that would knock him out all night. Before leaving the house, she made sure that Lil was asleep in the bed they shared.

As she walked, Aaelene felt the roots of the uneven path beneath her rabbit fur slippers and opened the laces of her cloak to let in the cold, clammy night air. The few nights a month she could get away alone like this were the closest she could get to feeling truly alive.

Through the hovering clouds, the moon remained constant. It would soon be the balance of light and dark for a merry meet. Everything was shifting. It would only take one moment to break this prison—one fleeting moment for the water to pour out and flush back in. Then, everything would be just as it was before, and she'd be free once more.

The textured shadows of black alder branches against the dull blue-white ice told her she'd reached the quarry. The ground fog had flattened all around it, and the petrified hemlock stuck out of the ice like a stick poking out of an orbital socket.

Aaelene inhaled the hard night air, picking up the scent of death through the trees. That decayed scent was everywhere on this island, on the kelp-littered shoreline, in bloodied pockets of the woods, and now, she could discern where it came from deep below the icy waters of the quarry. Hugh Robbins had himself an innocent death; therefore, it was a good smell, natural as rain.

In all of the time she'd been on the island, Hugh had been one of the few who had treated her kindly. It came from his genuinely good nature. Every time she'd entered the general store, she'd gotten no such charter from his wife, Roberta, or the other island women.

Aaelene closed her eyes and offered a plea to the Others of the springs, lakes, ponds, and rivers.

Máthair, lend me your protective arm.

I am your child. Keep me from harm.

Inspire me.

Give me the key that will open the gate.

Máthair, help me.

She pulled a tightly bound bundle from the cloak's deep pocket and removed her covering, laying it upon a granite slab. Naked, she shook off her fur slippers and walked across the ice toward the protruding fossilized tree. The crouching fog rose to meet her, encasing her body as the ice cried in distorted snaps and cracks.

The ice emitted one more horrible groan as the slush reached her ankles, sending off another small series of sharp cracks. The ragged dark hole surrounding the petrified tree began to open wider. In the ridge of ground fog, her figure fell below the ice.

SANDMAN IN ACADIA

Hans Krichels

Magnificent! The shoreline, the mountains, Great Head in the background.
Far away, the great pandemic of 2020 rages through the countryside.
It is late October now in Acadia National Park.
The beach is deserted—except for me (or so it appears).
Just below, someone has expertly carved a figure into the sand,
a muscled, middle-aged man with jowly cheeks and balding head,
sprawled on his back: Everyman awaiting his fate.
I stand, just above the figure's head, watching the waves roll in, lap at his feet.
Time and tide, they say, for no man wait.
Like sand through an hourglass, the toes wash away.
A swirling of frothy water, and the feet are gone.
Standing a bit farther back now, I document this process with my Canon
    EOS 1000.
Fugacia omnia, I think to myself, as the ankles and knees disappear.
Yes, all is fleeting, I repeat, but this at least I will preserve,
a creation of my own, overriding the best intentions of the artist before me.
I capture the sculpted belly as it dissolves into smooth, glistening sand.
And then, oh so smug in my godliness,
I look up and see to my left, high on a ledge on the path to Great Head,
a man with a tripod and a camera like my own,
capturing his own story of me and the story I am telling.
I look back to the figure at my feet. Only the tips of the ears remain
and the crescent dome at the top of the head.
I step back from the rising tide, the waves swirling and lapping at my feet.
Above me, the man on the ledge has vanished.
It is only me now ... and the gentle washing of the waves.

AT THE CROSSING

Kathleen Sullivan

When my Bob, my husband of fifty years, and I set out to hike the two-mile-long Morse Mountain trail through a forest of multistory pines and moss-covered rocky outcroppings toward Maggie's Beach and the ocean, the sun is so warm on our faces, the ground under our feet so muddy and smelling so fecund, it is hard to reconcile the date, Sunday, February 11, with the feeling that spring has arrived bestowing on us and the land all its generosity.

It has been years since we've walked this trail, which holds our memories of when we were a young family filled with optimism, of when our bodies were youthful and limber, and of a time before the catastrophic changes facing us and the earth were even a blip in our minds.

As I follow the path up and down its rolling hills, I feel a deep longing for those times, and beside that, a deep sadness, particularly when the trail opens onto the beach and we confront the once lush sand dunes, now deeply scarred by the force of the recent January storms.

After an hour or two of lying on the warm sand and scavenging shells streaked purple and orange and blue by the deft hand of nature, we head back to the car. Or we try to head back to the car. I hadn't considered the word "flood" on this blue-skied day or reckoned with the word "danger." But when we turn a corner, there it is: the trail over the salt marsh, which a few hours ago had been high and dry, is now awash in water.

A young couple who have just crossed the path from the other side warns us that the water is thigh-high and shockingly cold, the path underfoot unstable. They've taken off their shoes and socks and are waiting for the blood to return to their now bright pink feet.

The tide is still rushing in over the marsh, making its low burbling sound. Before us lies our altered world, I think to myself.

"I guess this is it," I say out loud to the couple, wondering what sense they are making of this moment.

"Yup," the man said, "this is the new normal. I'm from here and I've seen all kinds of changes in just the last few years. This marsh never used to flood. At least not like this. It's sad. And scary. There's a word for that. What is it?" he asks.

"Solastalgia," I answer.

"Yes, that's it," he replies.

Then we stand in the silence, witnessing.

Seven and a half inches. That's how much the sea has risen here in Maine in the last fifty years. Sometimes it's easy to dismiss that number, as I know the fishermen I talked to a few years ago up in Jonesport did. Normal, they called it. I wonder what they call it now that so much of that industry's infrastructure was destroyed in the January storms.

"Do you, like, do anything to address this?" I ask the couple, opening my arms to the earth. And there on the edge of the flood, she tells me her story.

Climate action has been her life's work. For many years, she was involved with 350 Maine. Now she works with a hands-on ecology center as well as with Maine Climate Action Now, the successor to 350. I tell her about the climate organizing work I do, and together we marvel that this climate hiccup, caused by an exceptionally high tide, brought us together.

Soon, a strong-bodied young man and woman arrive and begin to ready themselves for the trip across. It would be a good hour or two before the tide would recede, so my husband and I are torn about whether to stay or to cross. We are hungry and haven't brought any water with us, so we decide to cross and ask the couple if we could cross with them. In retrospect, I think our ask was too much. I am still sure-footed, but Bob, with seven more years on his birth certificate, is not, and the journey proves very difficult for him.

He needs support to keep from falling into the ice-cold water during the long crossing, and when the young man sees this, he puts his arm around Bob. Though it prolongs his own time in the cold water, this kind stranger eases him safely across. In another small, serendipitous gift from the universe, the man tells Bob he's a fireman and just the day before had been trained in cold-water rescues, so if Bob needs to be carried, he was prepared to do that for him.

This time we get safely to the other side, where about twenty people are waiting for the tide to go down. This time we have help. This time the risk was not too great. But the whole experience makes me wonder: what happens next time, what risks are ahead of us? And too, how much risk will it take for more people to join us in climate action, and what kinds of actions do we need to take that will make a difference in the ever-shrinking window of time that is left before we blow past not the once forbidden 1.5 degrees Celsius (which we've already exceeded) but the unthinkable 2 degrees Celsius?

WEDDING ON THE ROCKS

Hank Garfield

The wind felt chilly on Paul Bremerton's skin as he stepped out of the cabin and surveyed the tents, the mowed lawn, and the view out toward the open sea beyond the islands. The tide was in, and the water sparkled. His stepdaughter Gretchen, oldest of the four Sprauling sisters, had been blessed with a clear, crisp September day to get married.

The little blue sloop bobbed on its anchor. With a start, Paul realized that the dinghy was not attached to the boat's stern. Had Jeremy failed to secure it? But no, there it was now, with his stepson, Gretchen's older brother, at the oars.

"He's up early," Paul muttered aloud.

The breeze was onshore, pushing Jeremy along. And was that a car coming down the driveway?

The car pulled up beside the mini-camper parked behind the cabin, and a young man and woman got out. Paul recognized them from last night's pre-wedding dinner: Tom, the groom's younger brother and best man, and the small, dark-haired cousin, Elaine.

They wore matching navy sweaters and red windbreakers. Elaine carried a small canvas bag; Tom had a blue backpack slung over one shoulder.

"Didn't expect guests to start arriving so soon," Paul said.

"Jeremy's taking us sailing," Elaine explained, flashing a smile. "I've never been out in anything bigger than a Sunfish."

Paul tried to show no reaction. Jeremy beached the dinghy and hauled it up onto the beach. Elaine waved at him, and he waved back.

The civilized thing to do would be to invite all three of them in for a cup of coffee and try to convince them that this was a bad idea. But Elaine and Tom were already walking to the shore to meet Jeremy. The entitled firstborn, older brother of the bride, who had worked at a sailing camp all summer after his college graduation rather than looking for a real job, had somehow charmed his employers into lending him the boat at the end of the season, allowing him to come to Gretchen's wedding by water, just to show that he could.

Paul hastened to keep up with them. They must have cooked up this half-baked expedition at dinner the previous night. Jeremy stood by the dinghy. Paul saw that the kid had brought three life jackets.

"Jeremy," he said, "your sister's getting married at noon, and people are going to start arriving well before then." He looked at his watch to emphasize the point.

"Oh, we're only going out for a couple of hours," Jeremy said. "Don't worry, we'll be back in plenty of time."

"I don't like it," Paul said.

"It's not even eight," Jeremy countered.

"And by the time you get out to the boat, get the sails up, and hoist the anchor, it'll be eight-thirty. Then you've got to re-anchor and close the boat up when you get back. And then you've got to get dressed for the wedding. You're cutting it a little close."

But the damnable grin remained on the kid's face. "I'm not going to pull the anchor," he said. "I'll put the dinghy on it. All we gotta do is pick it up."

"I still think you should do this another day."

"Elaine and Tom are going back to southern Maine right after the wedding." The two guests nodded. "Come on, Paul, we'll be back in plenty of time. We'll take a couple of quick tacks out into the bay and come right back in. They just want a chance to get out on the water."

Their eager faces told Paul he was in a no-win situation. He had no real authority over Jeremy, and obviously, an appeal to common sense was lost on him. Nothing was to go wrong on this day. And perhaps nothing would. But this morning's sail was a wild card.

He looked hard at Jeremy. "You just make sure you're back on that anchor by ten o'clock," he said. "No later."

"Sure thing," Jeremy replied.

Paul wanted to slap that self-assured grin off the kid's face, but he held the dinghy as Jeremy's passengers climbed in. "Ten o'clock," he repeated as Jeremy dipped the oars and began rowing out to the boat.

Paul walked back to the cabin, scowling. Maybe his wife could put a stop to this. But when he told Annabelle, she said, "Paul, don't worry. It's a beautiful day, and Jeremy knows what he's doing. Besides, don't you think Elaine's kind of cute?"

She was matchmaking for her son on her daughter's wedding day. But he said only, "Yeah, I guess. I still don't like it."

"Everything's fine," she said as a truck rolled up onto the lawn. "Look, the caterers are here. Half an hour ahead of schedule." She smiled at him before dashing off to greet them. "Try to relax, will you?"

Paul would relax only when this day was safely over.

He wanted to go up the hill to his workshop and drink a morning beer. Instead, he walked the periphery of his six-acre property and wondered, not for the first time, what had possessed him to take on a woman with six kids.

But at precisely nine-fifty, the sail of Jeremy's boat reappeared around the point of Hog Island, and he breathed a sigh of relief. Maybe it was going to be okay after all.

Everybody else was up by then. Gretchen had arrived, and Annabelle and Madison, the next-oldest daughter, were helping her prepare in one of the back bedrooms. Madison's new boyfriend and daughter were playing with mussel shells on the front porch. A few members of the groom's family walked along the shore in their dress clothes; the younger Sprauling sisters pestered the members of the band as they unloaded their equipment. Their baby brother bounced a tennis ball against the side of the cabin, which would have annoyed Paul under normal circumstances. But he let it go and kept his eyes on the sailboat.

It passed the dinghy and tacked, and Paul watched as it sailed between the anchored rowboat and the shore. The people on the sailboat were waving; some of the wedding guests waved back. Paul saw that Jeremy, showing off for his audience, intended to take another close pass by the cabin, barely skirting the ledge that lurked beneath the surface. Though he had eaten a full breakfast, Paul's stomach gurgled.

Ted's parents walked down the hill from where they had parked. Paul saw that Margaret had her hair down but pulled partially back at the nape of her neck, held in place by a beaded leather hair clasp. Theo Addington wore a light blue suit and a tie. Paul, in jeans, had not yet dressed for the wedding. The two men shook hands.

"Couldn't have picked a better day," Theo said.

Annabelle emerged from the cabin to greet the groom's parents. She squinted out at her son in the sailboat, raising a hand to her eyebrows. "Isn't he awfully close?" she asked.

"Too close," Paul growled.

And then, just like prophecy, it happened. A crunch, audible from the shore, and the sailboat lurched and then stopped. He saw one of the figures on the boat stumble forward. The boat swayed but remained stuck in place. The sails flailed. He heard shouting voices.

"Oh, Jesus!" Paul exclaimed.

Ted's parents gave him a sharp look.

"What happened?" Margaret asked.

"He hit the fucking ledge," Paul said, quickly adding, "Pardon my language, but he's in trouble. The tide's going out."

Paul watched as Jeremy scrambled out onto the bow, grabbed the forestay, and leaned hard to first one side and then the other, trying to tilt the boat free of the rocks. Paul could see him exhorting his passengers to rock the boat. They ran from bow to stern, but the boat remained stubbornly stuck.

"Take down your sails and turn on the motor, you idiot," Paul muttered.

A moment later, Jeremy appeared to heed half of his unheard advice—he watched Jeremy go to the stern and begin tugging on the cord of the outboard motor. It roared into life on the third pull. Jeremy gunned the engine. The boat surged forward with a terrible scraping sound that made Paul wince.

He cupped his hands. "Put it in reverse!" he called out, realizing at the same time the futility of yelling over a revved outboard engine at this distance.

"Paul, you've got to go help them," Annabelle said.

"Jesus Christ almighty," he said through his teeth. "Of all the days ..."

He looked at his watch. Five after ten. If Jeremy hadn't been screwing around, he'd be on the anchor now, as they had agreed. But Annabelle was right. Paul had to move fast. If the little sloop didn't get off the rocks in the next few minutes, it would be stranded as the water seeped from beneath it and would remain there until the tide floated it again in six to eight hours.

Cursing, Paul power-walked up the hill to his truck, which he had parked beside the main house so as not to be in anyone's way. The keys were in it, as always, but someone had blocked him in. It took five precious minutes to find the owner of the late-model Toyota Corolla, and another three to get Paul headed out the driveway, carefully squeezing past the cars along the side. By the time he reached the public landing, rowed to his lobster boat, got the motor started, and cast off his mooring, Jeremy and his crew had been on the rocks for almost half an hour. They'd taken down the sails but were still trying to free themselves by using the engine and rocking the boat.

Paul turned on his depth sounder and headed out toward the stranded boat. Beyond it, Jeremy's dinghy bobbed at anchor, mocking them from deep water. When the depth dropped below ten feet, Paul cut back the engine and eased in. Eight feet, six, four and a half ...

"Do you have a line?" he called to Jeremy.

The kid cupped a hand to his ear.

"A line," Paul yelled again. "Throw me a line."

Jeremy nodded and hustled back to the cockpit. He opened one compartment, then another. Finally, he came up with a coil and tied one end to a cleat on the stern quarter. Paul slowly backed toward him, watching the depth sounder. Four feet, five again, three and a half ... close enough.

"Throw it," he yelled.

The kid gave him a lousy throw, but Paul was just able to grab one end of the line as it sailed past him. He cleated it off.

"Hang on!" he called back.

He aimed the lobster boat as directly as he could toward deeper water, putting himself at angle to the sloop. Slowly, he goosed the throttle. The line went taut. The sailboat lurched, scraped, moved a couple of feet, then stuck again with a hideous grinding. Paul felt his own boat tugged backward. He eased back on the throttle and slipped into neutral.

"Gonna try it from another angle," he called back.

But the sailboat had lost the race with the tide. Paul feared he might damage the boat if he kept trying.

He signaled to Jeremy that he was throwing back the line. Then he motored out to Jeremy's dinghy and tied his boat to the anchor line, cursing all the while, hoping that Jeremy had something substantial on the bottom. He got into the dinghy and rowed back to the sailboat.

"Shut it off," he said as he drew alongside. "You're not going anywhere."

Jeremy cut the engine. It quit with a cough of protest. Elaine stood in the cockpit, arms folded, her eyes like the blue ice that forms in the winter on the faces of roadside cliffs. She aimed them at Jeremy's back like steel blades, and even in this disaster, Paul was pleased to note that his stepson had lost his chance with this one.

"You got any bumpers?" Paul asked.

Jeremy nodded.

"Get 'em out. Get any extra life jackets too. We're gonna have to pad her as she settles. I'll take these two ashore and come back. Tom, you get into the stern. Elaine, you take the bow."

Elaine got into the dinghy gratefully, flashing one last poisonous look at Jeremy.

"Elaine, I'm sorry," Jeremy said from the tilting deck.

She tossed her dark hair back and looked toward the shore, her eyes glinty, blue slits in the sunlight reflecting off the water.

As Paul rowed, he contemplated leaving Jeremy out on the boat to fend for himself. It would serve him right. But what would he say or do if a rock poked a hole in the hull because Jeremy hadn't padded it properly? It wasn't even his boat, for crying out loud. But it was a boat in distress, and his disgust with Jeremy didn't abrogate his obligation to assist.

The wedding went off almost exactly one hour late, after Paul and Jeremy had braced the boat and padded the places where it would rest against the rocks, set out an anchor in deeper water, and rowed ashore and cleaned up. The small sloop had a forgiving shape. Its full-hull keel allowed it to rest at an angle; unless a stiff afternoon westerly whipped up a choppy sea, it would float without further damage.

But the damage to the day was done. By the time Paul took his place next to the bride in preparation for the ceremony, Gretchen was fuming.

"Well, he did it," she said. "He managed to make himself the center of attention at my wedding."

"Yeah, he has a talent for that," Paul said. "But you're the center of attention now. Smile, it's your day."

Just then, a chainsaw started up somewhere along the shore, or maybe out on one of the nearby islands.

"Oh, great," Gretchen said. "My day just keeps getting better."

She saw the groom and his brother waiting down by the temporary altar, backdropped against the sea and the emerging ledges.

She grabbed Paul's arm. "Tell the photographer not to get that damn boat in any of the pictures."

Author's note: An excerpt from the novel A Sprauling Family Saga *(unpublished).*

A ROGUE WAVE

Richard Foerster

This morning near my house, a wave swept up
a child from the rocks as she played. Soon all

the town's trawlers were pacing the sea's
long corridor, like family anxious for a ransom call.

Such a tiny window remained open at the end,
where the sun's needles made the sky flow red.

But we stayed, as if prayers could have sailed beyond
the unrelenting moan of the harbor horn. And later,

the air became glutted awhile with the earthy
stench of shells that the storm had washed

upshore and splayed across the rocks—innumerable
as the gathering gulls. So many wings

soared against those stony clouds. The ocean takes
its time. It yields, but somehow we hope for more:

to abstract from its surface the dream—
puncturing fact—the happenstance that can make

a mother, straitjacketed with fear, half-curse
the chantey of the waves that must bring

all loved ones home. And the gulls, as if to mock us
by example, waddled among the rich debris,

undeterred by grief. —I confess, I was hauled up
in their reverie as they rose with the few unbroken

quahogs razored in their bills and let them drop,
before their own plummet to a squabbling feast.

And when the sunlight finally clotted into black
and all but one boat came lumbering to port

and the birds departed for shelter against dark
and this night of neighbors sobbing, what was left

beyond the buoys seemed depthless as a stage, its scenery
struck, lit only by a klieg-lamp's narrow gaze.

THE SWIMMER

Ron Beard

This poem is dedicated to Puranjot Kaur, the swimmer, who made her second attempt to circumnavigate Mount Desert Island on August 3 to 4, 2021. Ocean temperatures hovered around 51 degrees Fahrenheit, and though she had the training and stamina that would have carried her all forty-four miles, the danger of hypothermia cut off her circumnavigation about halfway around.

Launching our kayaks from the cobble of Otter Cove,
navigating by memory and sound
      of waves' whisper against ledge
we set out in murky dark to find the swimmer

Off the point, we wait
      jostled by uneven swell
      big waves rucking up as they near shore
no horizon, nor friendly flash from Baker Island Light
we seem below the level of the sea itself

Milky sliver of moon distorted by haze
blobs of light where stars should shine
      produce a bobbing vertigo
exposed ledge mimics distant horizon
imagined mountains thrust up from the deep

And then, the flotilla:
puttering lead boat

green light to shore, red on seaward side
M.V. Osprey followed,
bright searchlight laying out the shortest line
accompanied by kayakers
one to lead, one to feed
      the swimmer between

We cut a wide circle
to come alongside the paddlers
relieving their watch
      every half hour a pause
      to hand off soup, hot chocolate
then off again
our pace constrained, matched
      to slow strong strokes of the swimmer

across the wide mouth of the cove
following spruce-capped shore
black against the night sky
waters calmer now
past Western Point and Hunters Head
past dimmed lights of the mansions
along Cooksey Drive
our focus divided
      between sea and swimmer

Progress punctuated by feeding stops
we make our way
      drawn to gonging of the buoy
      drawn to the white monument above
      waters that swirl along East Bunker Ledge

Dawn hesitant behind us
a cormorant swings close
      we hear the down beat of wings on humid air

darkness dissolves
revealing the welcome bulk
of Sutton Island
just before it vanishes in fog
seeming to swarm from the deep
and the lead boat slows
      so as not to lose the swimmer

A ghost sailboat rides at anchor
skeleton of a wooden dock
tethered to uncertain shore
roar of a lobster boat
passing unseen to our south,
now a shout, as kayak replacements
come up behind us
our four-hour watch complete
      as they feed the swimmer

      Soon we'll ask Captain Toby for bearings
      he'll consult his charts
      gesture to starboard
      through swirling white fog
      Sutton is right there
      once you get to the end
      set your course twenty-five degrees
      east of north

      We'll have to trust
      one lobster buoy at a time
      hugging the island 'til it corners
      we'll be left to the compass
      removed from the pocket of my vest
      nestled in the lap of my spray skirt
      aligning my boat with the bearing
      nervous energy we've held back

will scoot us forward at a faster pace
spectral gulls will emerge from gloom and pass us by
another lobster boat will loom
we'll pause to stay clear
while the sternman hauls a string of traps
sorts the keepers, restrings bait bags
we'll watch as the boat belches smoke
and we pass behind

On course
we'll spot the red can
marking entrance to Seal Harbor
thread our way through boats at anchor:
blue-hulled Hinckley, gold-winged sandal painted at the bow
restored passenger ferry, brightwork proud
battered aluminum skiffs on buoys
clean lines of Friendship sloop
silent as a graveyard
we'll paddle through to shore
my daughter and grandson wait
to hear our tale

For now, we pause and raise our paddles in salute
the lead boat heads into muffling fog
engine of *Osprey* growling aft

In between, still on pace
eleven hours through chop and swell
of cold Atlantic
heart, lungs, arms, legs
synchronized
to power her forward
    rhythmic splash of the swimmer

"Cove" by Leslie Dale Bowman

THE BLANKET THAT WARMS THE MEMORY

Greg Westrich

The woods were crammed full of fog. It felt like being inside an old stuffed toy. One of the squishmallows, Nemama, had been saved from her childhood. Emma had adopted several of them, which she still slept with. Even though she was sixteen. Even though she wasn't a kid anymore. Especially because Nemama was gone and Emma was on her own now.

The fog gripped the rough bark of the spruce trunks and snagged on the dead lower branches. It was tangled in the living crown of the trees. Not that Emma saw that. She could barely see her feet or the trail, much less the forest it passed through. She imagined a red squirrel sitting on a spruce branch. Ten feet off the ground, its tail curled up along its back. A cone gripped in its front paws. The squirrel paused in its meal. A bright green wave of moss moved through the fog. The green gently undulated as it moved past. The squirrel was frozen with anxious curiosity. It'd never seen moss fly before. The moss seemed to glow with its own light. The squirrel dropped the cone and scampered around the trunk, barking loudly.

Emma didn't hear the barking; the fog absorbed the sound before it traveled the twenty feet to her ears. On some level, though, she sensed it and turned to her left. All she saw was the blurred trunks and the white fog. Emma ran her fingers through her newly dyed hair. It was neon green, but she liked to think of the color as "damp moss in spring with filtered sunlight shining on it." That sounded more natural. She adjusted the straps on her day pack. In it was everything she'd need for two days in the woods. And two five-pound bags of compost. Emma was only planning this to be a day hike, but you never knew. She was on a mission. The compost had to be spread in just the right place. It was Nemama's last wish.

The trail rose gently, crossing barely exposed slabs of irregular bedrock. The fog made it feel like she was hiking through a forest of telephone poles. There was no green anywhere. Just muddy browns and deadfall grays. And the bright white of the fog. Off to her right, she heard a woodpecker peeling dead bark off a tree. The bark made a brittle thunk as it hit the ground. Black-backed woodpeckers did that instead of beating their heads against trees. Nemama told Emma that black-backs were never common, but as Maine heated up, they mostly headed north. Too bad it was too foggy to see the woodpecker. Normally, she'd wander off the trail to sit and watch the bird for as long as it let her.

Emma couldn't remember the last time she'd seen another hiker. Most trails were slowly being reclaimed by the forest, buried beneath blowdowns and hidden by new growth. Everyone was locked in their houses, plugged into the ultraverse. That's how she lost her parents. When they lost interest in everything real, she moved in with her Nemama. Emma had never been to school. She only knew that it used to be an actual place because Nemama explained it to her. Instead of plugging into the learning modules in the ultraverse, Emma learned from Nemama. They hiked and paddled and explored. Some days, they sat in the shade beneath a spreading oak tree in the yard and read books. Nemama called it decolonizing the mind. She also taught Emma important things like to call the people who invented the AI that ran the world "fucking tech-bros." Whenever she swore, Nemama looked guilty, but she never stopped.

The fog wrapped itself around Emma as she hiked on. It felt oddly warm and not wet at all. Usually, hiking through fog felt like taking a gentle shower. The trail began to drop gently, and Emma heard the hushed sound of the waves hitting high cliffs. It sounded like the sea was whispering to her. A green understory began to crowd the trail. Hillsides facing the ocean were always lusher than those facing away. It pays to respect your elders by looking at them and listening to their stories. And, as Emma knew, you learned about the world that way. The moss along the trail and the fir saplings knew it too.

The trail opened up beneath overhanging evergreen branches. The ground was rusty with needles. Clumps of moss clung to the exposed roots and the base of each trunk. Emma knew that beyond this soft, homey patch of ground, the trees ended abruptly atop broken cliffs that dropped nearly a hundred feet to the sea. A fin of rock called the Pulpit ran parallel to the shore with a narrow defile between it and her. She heard the surf sloshing around between the cliffs down there. A rough trail led out to the top of the Pulpit. Normally, that'd be her first destination—fog or no. But today she had a job to do that was a mile and a half down the trail.

Emma shrugged her shoulders and let her pack drop to the ground. She sat down and pulled out her water bottle. After taking a long drink, she lay on the soft ground. The heavy fog made the branches above her seem ethereal, smears of pale green floating in cream. She sighed with contentment and closed her eyes to listen. Nemama had shown Emma how to hear the stories the woods and water told, to listen with her animal self.

She felt something brush against her arm. It was soft, but cool. Neither animal nor plant. Slowly, she turned her head and opened her eyes. Small orange-red mushrooms caressed her. Odd, she thought, there was no breeze to make them sway. And besides, she hadn't noticed them when she sat down. She watched them for a minute. The small gelatinous caps atop chunky, red stalks moved as if alive, as if they were trying to tell her their story. Emma knew they were vermilion waxcaps. A common enough mushroom in the woods of Maine. But she'd never had them touch her before. Maybe they wanted her to tell them her story.

"Thank you for your story," Emma began. "But I'm on a mission today, so I can't stay with you. In my pack are two bags of compost—Nemama's remains that I need to spread on blueberry bushes atop a particular cliff."

The little mushrooms seemed to nod to Emma. "Nemama said burying dead people wastes space and burning wastes energy. So she wanted to be composted," Emma explained. When Nemama was young, only weirdos composted their dead, but for a long time now, the AI composted those who died. Their families created memorials on the ultraverse that they could visit. "Nemama wanted to feed blueberries where she went for her first backpacking trip. She was only four and didn't remember the details, but the view from where they put their tent was burned into her mind."

Emma sighed and stood. She swung her pack on and thanked the mushrooms again before heading down the trail. The trail turned away from the cliffs and passed through a patch of gnarled spruce. She knew the trail was crossing over a headland before the first pocket beach. She descended stone steps to the cliffs. The trail passed around the alcove that held the stony beach. She heard the waves moving the football-sized cobbles; they made a deep rumbling that seemed to hang suspended in the fog.

Across another head, the trail dropped down to the shore. The waves lapped at her feet as Emma crossed the smoothed bedrock and loose boulders. She climbed a rocky slope to a flat with views of a wide meadow that dropped down to the sea. Today, all she saw was the bright white fog. When she was six, she and Nemama had stopped here, marveling at the swaying grass and wash of pink sea roses. Emma described the meadow as magic.

"It is," Nemama agreed. "But there may be dozens of people in the ultraverse standing here and seeing this too. Except they selected mods. Some of them are standing here looking out over this meadow and watching unicorns cavort."

Emma looked at Nemama, who shook her head in disgust and added, "Fucking tech bros. People don't even know what's real anymore."

When they returned home, Emma put on her VR set to access school in the ultraverse. It was slow because she wasn't directly jacked in like most people who had implants in their brains. But she was able to find the Bold Coast. She teleported to the trailhead. No one drove anywhere in the ultraverse unless they wanted to. You just imagined the place, and you were there. People called it teleporting because of some ancient TV show. A menu popped up, offering to change the time of year, weather, tides, and—yes— even wildlife. Unicorns were a recommended mod, throbbing bright pink. That was the last time Emma ever visited the ultraverse. Nemama explained to her that people had become unable to tell the difference between what was real in the world and what was created in the ultraverse. Over time, they had forgotten there was a difference at all. Unicorns had become real because they existed in the ultraverse. What happened on the actual Bold Coast seemed to matter only to Nemama and Emma.

Lost in memory, Emma climbed off the overlook and crossed the meadow. She had to push her way through the waist-high grass, which scratched against her legs, but she barely noticed.

The trail climbed out of the meadow and back into the spruce. Many trees had been blown down in a recent storm. This always happened. The soil was shallow, so the spruce trees spread their roots laterally rather than deep.

As a result, when a nor'easter blew across the Gulf of Maine, trees toppled. Nemama said it was more common in Emma's lifetime than during her childhood. The trunks blocking the trail had been cut and cleared away. Fresh sawdust covered the ground and moss. The bright smell of recently sawn wood infiltrated the fog. Emma stopped to look at the cleared trail.

About the time Emma was born, the state had replaced trail maintainer crews with autonomous drones. They patrolled trails and kept them cleared of downfalls and repaired other damage. Most people liked the improvements to trail maintenance. But according to Nemama, others resented the loss of jobs and the intrusion of technology into their wild places. Drones weren't quiet. Groups formed to destroy the drones' charging nests. Over the years, Emma came across several downed drones in the woods. Once, she and Nemama had come across a broken solar panel and a burned-up nest. Shaking her head, Nemama said, "Fucking tech bros thought their technology could replace us." Emma reckoned they were right because they turned people into machines plugged into the ultraverse. She didn't say that to Nemama, though.

Emma ran her hand across the butt of a log at the edge of the trail. So long as the nest was intact, the drone working these trails could run itself almost forever. Even if there were no hikers left to hike. Even if most hikers in the multiverse thought unicorns were really here. As if there wasn't enough real magic here.

After a short climb past the recently maintained trail, Emma reached her destination. She stood atop a high cliff overlooking a cobbled beach where Black Brook emptied into the sea. The stream flowed out of the woods and disappeared into the cobbles. At low tide, the stream flowed out of the beach rocks at the base of a mass of broken black bedrock. Nemama said her dad and brother had spent hours climbing around on the rock while she played house with the cobbles.

Emma looked down from her clifftop perch but only saw the glowing white fog. She heard the cobbles grumbling as the waves pushed them around. Nemama's campsite was up a small rise away from the cliff. It was a flat dome of bedrock that prevented the evergreens from colonizing, surrounded by blueberry bushes. Emma knew exactly where the spot was because she and Nemama had camped there when she was six. Laying their sleeping bags next to each other right on the ground, they snuggled in and watched the stars come out after the sun set, making up names for the constellations they saw. At some point, Emma had fallen asleep listening to Nemama spin tales about the heroes in the sky.

Emma took off her pack and opened it. She took out the two bags of Nemama's remains, wiping a tear off her cheek. Opening one of the bags, she shook the compost out of it onto the bushes. She explained to the bushes why Nemama wanted to be here, how she hoped she'd nurture them and help them grow big, juicy berries in the summer. Tears were freely flowing down her cheeks. This time, Emma didn't wipe them away.

When she was done spreading Nemama's remains, she sat on the rock and let herself finish crying. She wept for the loss of her Nemama. She wept for herself all alone now. She wept for all the people in the ultraverse who'd never felt their legs ache or the caress of the fog on their cheeks. She left her pack at the old campsite and hiked down to the beach, stacking stones above where the brook slid beneath the cobbles. Then she clambered across the dark piles of irregular bedrock while the incoming tide lapped around the rocks, whispering condolences to her.

Emma lost track of time. The fog was thinning, and the sky was pale orange as much as white, suggesting the sun would set soon. And the sea had surrounded the rock she was on. She sloshed through the water to the trail. Her feet squishy wet as she climbed back to the campsite. Instead of grabbing her pack and heading back to the trailhead, Emma sat down and pulled out a bag of trail mix. As she munched, she realized she was going to spend the night here with Nemama.

She'd lie on the ground in her bivy bag and watch the fog dissipate and the stars emerge. She'd tell the berry bushes stories about the heroes and animal spirits that cavorted across the night sky. And she wouldn't be alone.

UNFOLDING

Marjorie Arnett

I feel a soft unimposing flutter
across my shoulders. Fairies
dancing the two-step, gliding
to a tune on a summer's eve.

Brahms Fourth Symphony floats
across the water, like sea-smoke
drifting indifferently toward frayed
edges of the bay.

The moon disappears then reappears.
I smell a storm coming, feel the quiet
knowing it will find its place. It is time
to move inside.

On the porch, an old Adirondack chair
offers comfort. I listen to first drops of rain,
feel cool air swirl as distant thunder warns
white caps will ride high along the coast tonight.

FIGURE OF SPEECH

Marcia F. Brown

This sun must be called *numinous*, these sea-smoothed

       stones deemed *indefectible*
rattling down receding foam. How
       we speak of a thing should honor it

for at least the length of our brief attention. Here
       a torn fish gapes, a gull's dashed skull
lies heavy and inert—over and over, the world
       at its most stunning and terrible

presents itself. I have grown accustomed
       to wonder, forgetting always
to live like a dead man, sick with longing.
       So distracted even now,

I nearly overlook the small and silver
       mound, motionless
above the wrack line. Pink perfect paws, fine nose,
       white whiskered muzzle—resting, as if

sunning on its back—dear
       little feet propped up, scrubbed nails
curled like a kitten. Unmutilated
       in any way, it seems—how dead?

Cliches swarm: Did he desert a sinking ship?
        Walk out coatless into a torrential downpour?
Betray his fellow gangsters? Find himself inextricably
        caught like himself, in a trap? In any case,

he is not what I pictured at all. I would not expect
        such sweetness. If he were plush—
a children's toy—I would want
        to nuzzle him. New to me

at close range, it is shocking how very much
        I like him at first meeting. How sorry
I am for all the black thoughts I have had
        about his kind. I ought to say a few words now.

And so I bow my head over the little rat body:
        Fellow creature I have so misjudged ... and so on,
until a feeling righteous and respectful takes its hold.
        Each day now, I will pause, I say. I will

pay honor to the smallest artwork
        of the firmament, speak meetly
to the humble elegance of animals. Knowing
        that I cannot. No more

than the living can know
        the chagrin of the dead, than the rich
are happy all the time, nor the cherished
        able to fathom the cold terror of the shunned.

FROM RIGHT HERE, IN THE SALT WIND

Patricia Smith Ranzoni

She wakes in their weathered ark knowing
there is something she needs to know how to put.
She fell asleep last night sure of it.

She steps out in the dark in just her smock
to ask night and day while they are here together.

Stands rooted as the coastal oaks in their frost-
scorched leaves until a knife of light unshells the east
and roosters up and down the bay cast hellos
not unlike morning gulls.

A howl not quite wolf sounds across the tidal brook
and dogs begin to bark back.

Glows switch on in the houses over the ledge
and the daylight shift heads to the mill.

She forgets she is cold with no coat.
Her eyes and ears and all she is sensing and learning
burn in the stirring of leaves still possessed of their trees.

She stands beholding, her arms bracing herself,
until a drop stings her grateful nose.
When she reaches out, a right smart rain touches back.
She dreams how this downeast sea pulled into the clouds
shawling this dawn. How this rain contains ancient news
from the voices dwelling in the shore rocks here.

She stays out gathering until she has her hands full
when, shaking, she huddles back in to put it down.

THE BENCH

Kate Kearns

at Monhegan Light

I sit to one side. A pheasant, its back
wrapped in five distinct patterns,

its silly crimson head, watches
from the berry bush. Sea on all sides.

I spent the day walking the island
the whole way round, more climb than hike,

uphill and down over rock and root,
honoring the narrow trail ledge, thinking

of you. Creamy brown doves
startled from their hidden nooks at my noisy heart.

You wouldn't have liked it. You preferred
the movies or a bar with gin and tall men,

manmade light between you and the eternal.
Legs complaining, I climbed up to the center

to watch the sun set over the Atlantic, to look
straight at the source through dark glasses.

When I close my eyes, a thousand blue suns
confetti my eyelids. You arrive with it, the sun,

dappled, warm on the cheek. Soon I'll turn
and the moon will be there, will have been there a while

on its slow upward totter. I'll lie on my back
and watch Venus appear, then one star, two, then

a crowd at the sky's open door.
At times, today, I felt like an abstraction.

Did you ever feel that way? Did you
ever stop, body spent, and wait for a breeze

to part the veil—below a yellow streetlight, perhaps,
or a high, moon-full window? Two truths

can rest side by side, their legs brushing
against each other. I miss you; you're here.

THE AUTUMN SWIM

JK McGann

I.
The sun is high and
bright for an October day
Standing on the beach
It might still be late July
Let's pretend for a moment

II.
Wading, then diving
No colder than usual
Deepest blue and green
Diamond sparks as I surface
It might yet be summertime

III.
But fall's cold breath says
No, as do the red-gold leaves
The season changes
Store this day, this swim, away
To hold fast again till June

"Whale Dust" by Leslie Dale Bowman

THE SEA: A DECKHAND'S VIEW FROM A SMALL COMMERCIAL FISHING BOAT

Nandiya Nyx

The world fell away
or, no, that's not right
the world became
endless swells
of deep green with ribbons
of white froth
Heads that
bobbed up   then vanished
sleek steely dancers
their bodies an arc
up! then a slide back into the
deep   as sure
and beautiful as anything

The sky cracked open
laid bare
holding us
telling stories
we'd only dreamt of
A panorama of forecasts—
A shift in wind direction:
      whispering to fish far below
      the water's surface
      driving them north and east
A rising wind:
      a fight with our lines

A driving rain at an angle:
        get those fish gutted and into the hold
        batten down the boat
        make haste to shore
The weather, pointing
beseeching
The current bargain on offer,
contracts paid out
in souls

And this: miles
and miles
and miles again: Water
        no land
        no cars
        no trees
        no bricks or concrete
        no other place just around the
        corner or
        down the road or
        the next state over or
        why don't we hop on a plane,
                just for a change of scene

How small we are!
Yet in the vastness
of this miraculous seascape,
we are everything—
or no, that's not right
more like
we're so much nothing
A delicious nothing
A sensing of balance
like the first footfall
after a too-long sleep

Repeated recalibration—
the way the body moves
when living upon
unceasing undulations
the extraneous falls away
        effortless
no catch in my breath
hair a mass of tangled salty threads
cheeks burnt in the
sun's salute

I say it was like this—
but in truth
each moment
there was a shifting
each swell smacking the hull—
a different timbre
some creatures visiting
        returning
others indifferent
        distant

When land passes away
people say there's an apparent sameness
People say the beauty of being at sea
comes in looking back toward shore

But I say
        Leave that familiar bank
        Let yourself be taken

For only in this
is return.

TRENDING INTO MAINE

Erine Leigh

Maybe we should thank the glaciers
For molding some batter of molten rock and fallen stars
Into this 3,400-mile shoreline,
Or maybe our thanks is meant for undersea eruptions
Causing this fissured edge of fingers and coves.

Maine's inlets and islands, its remote campsites,
Where fisherfolk and hunters, who
Hang damp red and black wool jackets by the hearth,
Strip off long boots,
May take up the pen
For moments of remembrance.

The great outdoors impresses them with the need for
An artist's sort of record-keeping.
But how to wrap this majesty into words?
Better to stand over the wood-burner stove, stir the chowder,
Check on the crock of baking beans, move the salt pork to the top.

HANDS TOGETHER

John Reinhart

I go to the water,
            tides going in and out, breathing
     to maintain   balance,

                  blood of the world, waving
                      to trees

along   the   shore,   breathing

           in and out,
                dip
                my
                toes

as I once dipped fingers   in the font upon entering

the chapel,
this chapel
       open to all,   vaulted heavens

above,
sunlight, starlight, lightening our burdens

if we let go,
go to the sea,

let the water cleanse

our feet,

let the salt remind us
where we are, where
we will return

PADDLING THE MARSHES

Erin Covey-Smith

You like to think you have a deep inner life,
but you don't: all is laid bare to the world.
To have a soul is to be diaphanous. Skin is nothing
if not permeable, a heart nothing if not tide-driven.
We're passing through permanence, and it passes
right on through us.

Canoeing the back marshes, egrets and herons
like pterodactyls (they have the bones of dinosaurs—
what do *you* have within?) alighting in briney trees;
the grasses cow-licked every which way from high waters;
an azure flash of kingfisher; sonant stir of salt water.

That tug inside, the longing pull, is this tide here, churning
through channels, pulsing blood slow, breathing your breaths, in
and out. And in the furthest backwater before the brittle-boned pine
leaning ancient over the banks—silence of no roads, no planes.

It could be three hundred years in the past,
or tomorrow.

THE MESSAGE IN A BOTTLE

Douglas Wright

Your toes fry on the cracked asphalt, finding the cool spots on the white lines as you dash from the back seat to the path, no concern for breaking your mother's back. Out-of-staters littered the sandy beach, so your father drove the extra twenty minutes to the local cove, accessible to everyone but not really. Children's screams fade in and out, the cathedral walls of the cove echoing the waves and voices up the cul-de-sac, its baritone hum a gravitational constant.

Parents having installed themselves on the sliver of damp and dank sand, books in hand and bottles of beer sweating beside them, you and your brother start exploring. Scrabbling from stone to stone, your summertime calluses as protective as any boot against the slick granite and razor clams.

Playing with some rockweed, its bubbles slippery and twisted, they resist your attempts at popping them. Failing one, you try others, a couple relenting, their bodies hiss and rupture, little spiral galaxies of foam dance down your forearm. The smell is evocative, like cherry blossoms in bloom or a dog in heat, all of it a taboo to your young mind, so you wipe your hands on your thighs and climb drier boulders.

Screams. Your brother's. Your parents' books drop an inch.

"Over here. Quick!"

Books returned to noses, you jump and climb back a few yards to where your brother is standing; a sandy crater melts at his feet, an upturned stone at its side.

"It's enormous!" he exclaims, sandy, water-logged finger outstretched.

Among the polished stones, its hind legs wriggling, tearing at the drying sand, lies a crab green and angry at the disturbance. Grabbing it, legs latching onto your fingers, a moment's fear passes as you each gauge the other. Your brother screams in delight as the crab salivates, slowly asphyxiating in the alien world. It raises a pincer, ready to defend itself against the cackling Titans. You laugh.

After shoving it in your brother's face and him tumbling backwards, you bring the crab near. From your whirlpools to its jeweled quasars, eye to eye, life recognizes life, and you dance in the shared existence. The diminutive grandeur of the very act arrests your breath as you tumble past an event horizon into a singularity of communion, but the moment is cut short. A meteor shower of sand pelts your backside; the pain travels up your hamstrings like a whip midcrack to your shoulder blades. Turning, your brother's face wavers between righteousness and fear.

Chasing him, your high-pitched squeals echoing out into the eternal seas, your orbits spin tighter and tighter, his feet slide out, screams and laughter blend in the descent. Where there is a you was a nothing, a preexistence that rests outside time and space and laughs and stones.

In your nothing, not before, quantum perturbations spun and plucked their polydimensional strings, their movements rising and falling, cascading into themselves till a resonance was reached and from that potential came all—you, him, the stones, even the green crabs. As caught in the strafing beam of a lighthouse, tsunamis of the very foundational forces that define our universe erupted, crested, and crashed into existence, the mists rising, billowing into the unknown through seas of light and heat. And as our place stretched and formed, cooling into a three-dimensional space enveloped in some higher-dimensional seafoam, forms and structures emerged as clearly as the carved sands in the wake of undertow.

Gravity took it from there, pulling, crashing, and spinning great whirlpools, creating maelstroms of matter that boiled under their weight. In that chaos bloomed the first stars. These leviathans, swimming in seas of hydrogen gas, took up more space than the orbit of our future Earth. Mass and the dark depths of gravity inexorably crushed them to nova, their upturned and distended abdomens rupturing, spilling out their entrails to the sound of gulls and the eternal hum of the cosmos. Following their tumult, the successive generations made do with the matter ejected from their ancestors' starfall. A seething foam of starlight, star bright, dripping down the forearm of eternity.

Eons passed, not a crab in sight, but the elements that would be crab started to form in the bellies of the stars—calcium, carbon, copper, oxygen, metals, gasses, bases, alkalines. All were consumed by the next generation of stars or cast out to the black seas of space to cool, aggregate, and start their own slow facsimiles of star formation into rocky little bodies. As that brume cooled and folded into itself, violently churning into miasmatic regolith, as a stone is tossed into a still water, a new star blossomed. Its brilliance eschewing all of the interplanetary gases and lighter bodies, tossing them to the very limits of our solar system into an enveloping coastal cloud with plenty of chop lying in between.

Within this newly formed tide pool, the clockwork machinations of our heavenly bodies ticked away. The classics, the godly—Mercury, Venus, Mars, Jupiter, and Saturn—as well as those no less stately but obscured by time and distance, lost in the murky depths of our little expanse—Uranus, Neptune, and the innumerable asteroids, dwarf planets, comets, and moons—all spun and circled each other in one grand fest noz. As the partners neared and parted, arms embraced, spirits high, asteroids tumbling into place, comets' tails as proudly raised as any peacock's, the car's wipers swished near and far, wiping away the crystalline ejecta of the passing comet. The summertime bugs are in full force, and you watch their entrails arc across the windshield. Lower back stiff from the drive, you twist and reseat your bum.

After the monotony of I-95, each turn here is an assault, an erasure of your memories. Chains of pharmacies, fast-food restaurants, motels, and grocers had fallen from orbit, their combined mass pulling others nearer till all the quaint gables and teenagers slinging insults had been replaced by metal flashing and SUVs. You keep expecting to see the old weather-beaten shops, paint chipping and exposed wood patinaed a silvery gray, like a child had come along and filled the spaces with their pencil, or the rusted-out trucks, more Bondo than steel, sputtering their fumes underneath labor-hardened men. But they're no more, mere echoes remaining in street names and Polaroids peeling in the attic.

Crossing the bridge, while suppressing your irrational fear of it collapsing, you smell the rotten-egg stink of the low tide mixing with the manufactured sting of diesel, and you're brought back to your youth—bent over, raking the bay for clams with your grandfather, searching for bubbles in the sand.

Tossing the reverie aside, you reason with yourself, it's the traffic that's most upsetting; speed limits are now the minimum, the roads have been widened, and traffic lights dot the town, as garish and crowded as the family buoys in the bay. It all stands in the way of the town remembered. Laboriously, your husband rounds corners and still manages to hit the sidewalk with the trailer. You stifle a snicker.

Still, you shouldn't be surprised at the changes. You've watched your town shift and change through the tides of time—fires, estate sales, divorces, and parking lots. Even when you'd found yourself pulled away, in search of work or self, you had need of traveling back up here. Each hungover drive back from a wedding, each wake, as your throat wound round itself in grief, each farewell to friends and families now bound only by the line of failing memories, had you pass these same buildings, these same roads, and watch your once-home change hands and get renovated or flattened—get changed.

Eyes falling, you follow the purple worm, the scar tissue that had been hooked permanently sutured across your husband's new knee, and you think upon how much his strength has diminished. Catching yourself, you bury such maudlin thoughts in a quick nuzzle and a sigh; he pretends not to notice.

The cottage is dark, musty, and carries the shroud of having been vacant for many months. Weeks before the grandkids arrive, you have time enough to dust, change the traps, and unload the trailer full of supplies, most of it gifts. Right now, though, after a full twenty-four hours behind the wheel, true-crime podcasts, and the AC never being "right," you want a glass of wine, a couch, and a blanket.

Taking an e-bike to the cul-de-sac in the dawn light, your knee not up to the walk unassisted, you find the concrete access slope gone, effaced by time and finances, and briefly you envisage the desire path of your youth, beaten into the earth by generations of briny bare feet. In its stead, blocking the view, rests an empty—home isn't the right word—estate, bound by wrought iron that had metastasized its way onto the coast. Still, the heartbeat of the cove reaches out, as does the memory of a green crab and a long-since-deceased brother's squeal of joy.

Peddling over to the crowded public beach, you find a spot at a picnic table, its surface sticky and jagged, and enjoy an ice cream and watch, smiling, as the young families spill out of their cars, the parents savor the singular moments of silence, and the children shudder from the thrill of sugar before tumbling back into their out-of-state boxes.

A child cries out, you turn toward the parking lot, and overhear the mother refusing their pleas. The cries rise, then fall, and the young boy whimpers to the curb. With seawater-spiked hair and tears streaming, he unburdens his swim trunks, builds a little cairn out of seashells, polished stones, and sea-glass. Atop the pile he places, reverentially, the desiccated remains of a crab. You smile and swallow away the knot in your throat.

You go back and curl up against your husband watching nothing on the TV. The crab remains. And it might rest just so for eternity if it weren't for the waves. Ceaseless, the waves hadn't noticed the arrival of life or crabs or humanity. Following the moon's lead, its gravity pulling at the briny coat-tails of its captor planet, the tides slosh near and far. Coupled with the sun's uneven heating that stretches and tears at the atmosphere till great storms are extruded out and, finding the balance between hot water and cool air, spun across the globe in fantastic Coriolis arcs, the coasts are battered, reshaped, and changed.

The sun will set and rise, and the emptied carapace will have been washed, imperceptibly beaten a little smoother. Gulls will fight over it, tear at it. Its pieces broken, marooned, and worn to calcified flakes of not-quite-sand or rescued by the next child searching for treasure. Either way, it will return to the Earth, worn down by tidal forces and time. And you'll return alongside it, as will humanity.

Through society and individuals, humanity will reach for eternity or at least for tomorrow, and despite the millions of years of evolution and the fictions they've told themselves, they'll eventually fail. Either marooned on island Earth, obscured behind a fog of asteroids and short-sightedness, or even out "there" island hopping between the stars. Time and tides will not relent. With humanity or after, the stars will eventually burn through their fuel, and there will come a day when the last star shines and fades and turns black as an abandoned lighthouse. Radiation will continue to boil beneath the skins of these "dead" stars. Blackholes and iron stars will hum and glow in light frequencies too extreme for our meager eyes. And more years will need to pass than there are grains of sand across all of Earth's beaches before even the very forces that made matter possible enter their twilight years, with bad knees and melancholic memories. The nuclear and strong forces—the mortar between the atomic bricks—will shake, hum, and relent, decay as coastal stones on legion worlds, and fall into a dark, seething foam in a sea of quantum potential. In that effervescence, bubbling to the surface for a few scant decades, had been you. Time enough, but just, to delight in shared existence before having to take in one last look of your bedroom, at your brother or your child, slowly breathing nearby before your eyes, heavy with the day's tasks, fall and the warm embrace of dark nonexistence consumes you.

In those turbulent waters of time and matter, the universe saw fit to know itself through you, however briefly, to dip your hand into the cool, temporal waters of eternity and have your reflection stare back, framed in the compound eyes of a green crab.

TASTING FOG

Deborah Pfeffer

Fog lingered on my dampened pillow and in my waking mind. I rubbed sleep from my eyes and took a deep breath of fresh July air flavored by the scent of pine. I usually enjoyed the liminal place between dreams and waking, but something was playing with my mind, and I couldn't figure out where I was. I could hear crashing surf, and through a thick curtain of fog, a huge boat was aimed for our bow.

From my safe, still bed in the vee berth, I could see Charlie sitting in the cockpit of the *Bacchanal,* and I wondered who was sailing the boat. Sun glittered off the brass coffee grinder he was holding; Charlie was giving the handle quick turns. As I became more fully awake, the frightening dream became a memory of a very real experience the day before.

"Anchors down. We got a good hold." Charlie craned his neck to peek at me and smiled. "Coffee will be ready shortly. Come on up."

I struggled out of the sleeping bag, stepped down from the vee berth, and climbed the ladder, squinting in the bright morning light.

"Where the heck are we? And why do I smell Christmas trees?"

"Roque or broke." Charlie repeated the oft-quoted phrase of sailors who dream of reaching Maine's fabled Roque Island. Like most places that hold some enigmatic specialness, Roque is remote, and to reach it takes determination. These are the places I like best. Resorts with their pool boys and heated towels—not so much.

"Ohhh!" I picked up a small cushion and hugged it as I sat companioned to morning stillness. Less than fifty feet away lay an uninhabited white sand beach that had to be at least a mile long. Layers of spruce trees stood behind, a perfect background.

"Honey, I feel dazed. When I went to sleep last night, we were underway in dense fog, and I wake up to this."

"Paradise all right. After yesterday, this is pretty damn good," he said.

"I just had a nightmare about it! A huge boat was coming right at us. There were humongous cliffs and big waves crashing all around us. When I woke, I couldn't tell if it was real or just a dream."

"Oh, it was real alright." Charlie had finished grinding the coffee beans and was pouring boiling water over the grinds and into the insulated Melita pot. "I'd read the guidebooks. They all warned of strong magnetic anomalies around there. That stretch of coast near Acadia where we were yesterday, just off Schoodic Point, is really dicey."

"Well, the afternoon fog didn't help. Honestly, I could barely see the bow." I was remembering it all as it really happened.

"It rolled in fast. When I felt I couldn't rely on the instruments, I knew I'd have to rely on dead reckoning and started looking for any visual through the fog. I took a position at the last buoy and replotted our course to the next waypoint from there," Charlie said, priding himself on his navigation skills.

The smell of freshly brewed coffee, the sound of water lapping against the hull, and the tranquility surrounding the *Bacchanal* were in direct contrast to the terror I awoke to moments ago. I still had shivers from the dream. Pouring the steaming coffee into the cobalt blue cups helped keep me right here, safely anchored in sunlit seclusion, by this idyllic beach.

"Something sure was off. We certainly were off course." When I spoke, it must have sounded like criticism because Charlie was quick to reply,

"The set of the current must have been stronger than I thought." He abruptly went below to fetch half-and-half.

The scene from yesterday afternoon came flashing through my mind, and I relived bits of it.

We had entered a dense fogbank, heard the waves, and knew from our plotted position on the chart we shouldn't be close enough to shore to hear them crashing. Sound was dispersed in the fog, so we weren't confident of what course change to make. An immediate decision had to be made. Charlie pushed the tiller to port, pulled the sails amidships, and increased power on our 15-hp Yanmar inboard engine. We knew it was clear to our stern and prepared to reverse direction. As we did, pink granite ledges appeared, looming in wispy air high above our mast. Mighty Atlantic waves smashed and sprayed against them with tremendous force. The *Bacchanal*'s engine roared as we pulled away from the cliffs. It happened so quickly my feelings hardly had time to acknowledge the terrifying danger.

The Atlantic is indifferent, the weather in Maine is changeable, and we were not out of it yet.

"Take the helm. I have to recalculate our position."

As I squinted into the gray curtain beyond the bow, Charlie went below to the nav station and a dry chart. The crashing sounds were less audible, and I loosened my grip on the tiller. Fog alters visual perception, and a buoy can appear as big as a boat. At first, I thought what I was seeing off the bow was a buoy or bell appearing out of the smoky mist. I was wrong. One long and two short blasts of their horn, and the bow of another sailboat appeared. I steered ten degrees starboard to indicate I saw it and was adjusting course. The other boat did the same. We passed port-to-port just missing a head-on collision. Close. Too close.

"Here you go. Swirled not stirred," Charlie said, grinning topside, to join me, my coffee fixed just the way I like it. I don't go for the quick stir. I'd rather pour the cream slowly and watch patterns appear.

Looking back to shore for reassurance after being in the memory, I was stunned. Galloping along the curving, crescent beach, two people were riding horseback, one horse chestnut, the other white. In the rolling meadow behind the dunes, deer grazed in magnificent sunlight.

"This whole scene is just dreamy," I said as much to myself as to Charlie, still looking at the horses on the beach.

"This is the world I want to live in—what's right here and yesterday's impenetrable fog. I will never forget this."

And I never have. I'm not a painter. In my lifetime, I've painted two little watercolors. One of a sailboat seen through a mist, the other of this beach at Roque Island. They rest together on my drafting table, waiting to be finished.

I don't remember what else we talked about that day, as we sat snuggled on the port settee, looking to the beach. I do remember how rich the coffee tasted, how yesterday's fog, this beach, spruce trees, riders, horses, sun, and silence were in it. It tasted like all of that.

DREAMS OF DROWNING

Kristen Lindquist

My ocean swims with lobsters, sharks, seals, boats chugging off into the cold blinding light of dawn. I have leapt off a bridge into the cloying arms of kelp, dissolved with the salt on granite cobbles. I wait, legs scarred by barnacles, limpets clinging to my fingertips, for waves to leap into dolphins' backs. But the sea never gives anything away.

opening a window
onto distant islands
childhood fears

SHIFTING VIEWS

Ellen Goldsmith

1
Sea smoke covers everything
Just the treetops are visible

I can't see what I know is there—
not an erasure but an opening

into another view
Time stands still

2
I woke in the middle of the night
to the brightest gibbous moon at its full extent

Do the phases of the moon know each other
offer greetings in passing?

3
The beauty of ice
along the shore amazes me

I can't find the words to hold
the fractured shapes

their sheen and mystery
I say frozen water

CHANNEL BLACK

Valerie Lawson

Inlet the way a river does: the mouth
a black dog lapping a bowl of stars.

The same kid always wins, shows up
in the right wrong places, another makeshift

town tucked in his pocket. Fog, that thief,
unravels the landscape, changes the rules,

watches the bank chase an orange dog, a crown,
a boat with a single oar, a bigger boat, the rising tide.

BAKER ISLAND

Ron Beard

Whale oil powered the light
thrown twenty miles round
by Mr. Fresnel's faceted lens
It turned in a clockwork
wound every four hours
forty-two stone steps up
     to tower's top

The one time it broke
lightkeeper Robbins turned it by hand
slow, steady
to keep the beat of light
to keep boats safe
     over two whole nights

Now, the keepers are gone,
some to the graveyard
with a view of hump-backed mountains
across the water
     or scattered to homeplaces elsewhere

William Gilley was the first keeper
and first settler, raising
with his good wife Hannah
     six sons and six daughters

Big families a good strategy
for life on a small island
plenty of hands
to plant gardens in stingy soil
        fortified with seaweed, stove ash, fish guts

Self-sufficient
chickens
Leicester sheep
a Devon milk cow
freshened with a yearly visit
        from a bull in a dory

They sent off wool, flax,
wheat for milling on the mainland
brought home cloth, flour
cash money
        for churned butter, cod and haddock

Government pay helped for a time
'til a Whig was elected President
in eighteen twenty-eight
Democrat Gilley declined
        to keep their Light

Eighteen keepers over a century and more
some with their families—
wives timed their walk across sand and mud
over the bar at low tide
to reach the midwife
on the next island
        in time

Some were bachelors
tending their solitude

or courting the teacher
at the tiny schoolhouse
  built before the nineteenth century turned twenty

Baker Island Light flashes white
every ten seconds
six beats of the heart
matching my breath in and out
a pulse of comfort across the sea
  when I wake in the night

Coast Guard automated the works
in nineteen fifty-seven
a lens of plastic now, sun powered.
  The whales are glad.

Author's note: With appreciation to the diligence of Cornelia J. Cesari for her monograph/history of Baker Island.

THE DICTIONARY OF STONE

Cynthia Reeves

Long ago, a stonemason knelt knee-deep in shoreline intertides
and sucking mud on the living side of the Megunticook, tracing veins
into patterns, shaping boulders into blocks with hammer and chisel,
feather and wedge, song of metal on stone, wedding cut rock
to cut rock, ice water sluicing over his numbed hands. The quay
rose and rose, contained the untamed falls, and remains, yet unnamed.

Today, a lone fisherman awake before dawn stands on this same quay,
fixes a bright, feathery fly to a barbed hook, casts his line, one
flowing flash of steel slivered through blue sky. Newborn sun
splinters the water, pulsing shattered rhythms of light as the last ash
of the fisher's morning cigarette drifts into the bay. That is all—
all the day the day makes until the pole shudders, bends, nearly

breaking, and he reels and pulls, reels and pulls, marks time as
the cod rises, unburdened by the sea. Fish-scales fire in daybreak rays,
the codhead slammed against the long-gone mason's dam then cut
from its body, fishmeat cased in shaved ice. The blunted head lies silent,
its unblinking eye a passage to nowhere and everywhere, its mouth
mouthing one final O—surprised, it seems, by the cold weight of stone.

"Enchanted Forest" by Don Peterson

WHAT REALLY HAPPENED ON BOON ISLAND IN 1710

Christopher Packard

October 31, 1722
Overheard at the Pepperrell Tavern
in Kittery, Province of Maine:

"We ate him. He died, and we ate him—a human man. Aye, so don't talk to me about being hungry and forlorn. The poor fellow gave out on us and died right there on that pile of rocks. He was the ship's carpenter, he was. But we didn't have a ship no more. No coats, no shelter, no food. And that shit-sack of a captain, he says we've got to eat him, or we'll all end up dead like him. Says it was no sin—we didn't kill him. 'It was providence,' he says. We raised a commotion, sure, but deep down we knew—maybe he was right. We were cold, starving. We'd been there two weeks, maybe more. Christmas, it might've been. I don't know. So Captain Deane goes and cuts off the dead man's head, his hands, and his feet, and flays him—so he won't look human, I suppose. He brings back strips of fat and meat, wrapped in rockweed, dipped in the sea. We ate him. What else were we supposed to do?

"Don't look at me like that. We weren't alive, and we weren't dead. We were somewhere in between. Only our souls held our skin to our bones— there was nothing left of us. My toes were black, my fingers numb. All we could do was huddle under that flapping scrap of sailcloth we'd turned into a tent. Most of us were too weak to walk. With no fire, we couldn't even melt the frozen sea spray the wind carried over that sliver of land. But Boon is no island—it's a craggy ledge, barely pokes its head over the waves at high tide.

Nothing lives there, just the sea. It's part of the same ledge that wrecked the ship. The captain was at the helm as we sailed into a tunnel of snow and wind. That little ship was tossed like a toy. It was a perfect night to lose her. The *Nottingham Galley* hit the ledge and stuck fast. The waves drove us further on and pitched us to listing until we had to abandon her before she broke apart and the sea claimed her. All fourteen of us made it out of the water that night. But there was no time to take supplies.

"On clear days, we could see the mainland. We knew the town there had warm hearths and safety, just six miles away. But it might as well've been the moon, for all the good it did us. We built a raft—the carpenter did—but the seas were too rough and the water too cold. It took the raft and two men with it. Time wore on, and we wore out. Our prayers were for naught. Did nothing. Captain Deane was a brute—quick with his fists and boots—but he was right. The food was gone, and the sea gave us no more mussels. Islands like Boon aren't land, and they aren't sea. They aren't safe, and they aren't dangerous. They're where the fates decide what else they'll take. The first one they took was the cook. Maybe he, and the two lost to the sea, were the lucky ones. Not me, and not the carpenter. None of us who got rescued were lucky. Is a cannibal still a man?

"No, I don't want your pity—no more than I'd set foot on another ship, or build a house on Boon. But I'll take a bite of that beef, and that bread—if you've got some to spare."

Author's note: This flash fiction is based on true events that occurred in 1710 in Maine, near the town of York. Boon Island remains the most well-known place in Maine with documented cannibalism.

THE TRADE

Cathy McKelway

The grudge was heavy inside the pocket of her T-shirt, warm against her chest. She climbed into the rowboat, tucked a shovel under the middle seat, and pulled into the harbor. Lobster boats sloshed and rocked. Hardware rang against the mast of a lone sailboat and the night smelled of cold ocean. At the town landing, she checked her watch, tied up, and climbed out into the night.

Long ago on a similar night, under a waning moon, her grandmother, old, wild-haired, and strange, had conjured a wart away. The suburban crossroad where her grandmother conjured was nothing like the one the woman walked to this night. Dogs had barked from backyards. The blue light of a TV showed through a fence covered in vines.

This midnight crossroad had a fenced-in boat storage area with a theft-deterrent light on a pole on one corner. The rest was crowded by woods and thick with darkness. She checked her watch—midnight. The grudge in her pocket had nothing to do with her grandmother or the wart, both long gone, but the woman hoped similar magic on a similar night would eliminate the grudge as her grandmother's conjuring had rid her of the wart.

Her grandmother'd had a ham bone in her pocket that midnight long ago. She'd taken it out and gestured to her granddaughter to take her shoe and sock off. The woman remembered how cold her foot, the one with the wart, had been. Gran rubbed the bone on the wart and gestured impatiently for the shoe and sock to go back on. "The Old One trades at midnight," she'd said. "You give something, you get something."

The woman took the grudge out of her pocket and admired it. Smooth. Flecked with colors. She'd had it many, many years. It'd made her life worth living *and* sucked it dry. Before her watch ticked 12:01, a voice spoke from the woods. "Do you have a cigarette?"

The woman closed her eyes until they were sightless, opened them, and looked into the deep darkness. Tree shadows cast by the almost full moon fell across the road. The voice came from somewhere and nowhere. "A cigarette?" it rasped.

The hairs on her neck rose. She pulled the wool cap over her ears. "I don't smoke," she said. "Never did." Her words came out strong, not whispered or tinged with fear, though her knees were weak. She tried to think who might stand in the cold and wait for her foolishness. Her husband has been dead these past five years. She had no children.

"Pity," the voice said with a sigh.

The woman took the grudge in her right hand, rubbed it over her heart, then on her head, in case it lived in synapses and folds beneath her skull. She held the grudge up into the moonlight in the direction of the gravelly voice that might or might not be a figment of her imagination.

"I give this to the Old One to sell, bargain, or keep. I give it for free, I will not plant it deep."

That was all she remembered of the words her grandmother'd used. The girl she was back then had hidden her face in her hands, and put her fist in her mouth to stop a scream that rose from her chest when a shadow came out of the night to scrabble and scratch in the dirt where her grandmother buried the ham bone at the long-ago crossroad.

One word, a laugh, any sound, no matter how small, will break the deal, Gran told her before they left the house. "You'll be stuck with that wart until some fool doctor cuts it off, and then, it'll grow back. You've got to conjure them right and permanent. He's got uses for warts. He always takes them."

The woman never saw a wart after that without wondering how it got on someone's nose, cheek, or eyelid. She didn't know what her grandmother got in trade. They hadn't spoken about the conjuring. Ever. She hadn't wanted the wart back.

The woman stuck the shovel in the ground as close to the center of the crossroads as she could; the dirt was hard-packed. She barely got the grudge covered when a cloud crossed the moon, and the night went black. She shaded her eyes so she could only see her feet and hurried away. She might have seen what scrabbled in dirt, digging and huffing, but she didn't look back.

The grudge had been her friend for many years. It had excused failures, explained losses, opportunities missed, lovers sent away, and children that were never born.

Fog came across the harbor while the woman rowed home. Opaque clouds wet her face and hands, swallowed the oars, and muffled every sound. Her house was dark, but she knew the way, across the harbor and up the rocky path. She turned on the lights, lit the woodstove, and went searching. She knew cigarettes were in the house somewhere, stale and unsmoked since her husband's death. It took her an hour to find them on the workbench in the garage. In his armchair, by the fire, she lit one and inhaled. Crossed her legs. Ahhh. So good. Someone or something made off with her grudge, and she was dying for a smoke.

AT HUNTERS BEACH

Catherine Schmitt

Winter ends early, ice and snow melting, rain falling, moving through the forest, into water.

From the steep, spruce-clad cliffs and slopes of Cadillac Mountain, Hunters Brook carries a season's worth of carbon downstream. Invisible now, leaf and twig have disintegrated, into the water and into the bodies of mayfly, snail, and minnow.

The brook winds through ravines, eroding and undercutting banks, pulling spruce and cedar into the water with each flood. Some trees have broken and fallen across the channel, which braids around patches of gravel. One reach of the stream is completely buried by fallen trees. So much wood in the water can seem messy, like a problem to be solved. But wet trunks collect bacteria, fungi, and algae, a grazing ground for invertebrates. Fish shelter in the shadows of fallen branches. Logs jam and redirect the current, creating new riffles and pools: habitat complexity. Historical records, and the evolved ecology of aquatic life, suggest that streams once contained much more wood than they do now.

As wood gets waterlogged, it starts to fall apart. Always, it is moving downstream.

The brook levels out, a straight run to the sea, but then vanishes into a hill of smooth, rounded stones, anchored by driftwood. The water emerges and fans out across the rocks and wrack lines of seaweed. Forest carbon and aromatic terpenes meet the tang of iron and salt. A loon calls from the water, somewhere out beyond the diamond flashing of sun on waves.

The beach is strewn with wood, barkless and bleached. Eroded earth and piled debris mark the height of last year's flood. The force of water uprooted shrubs and trees and battered rocks against the bark of other trees, leaving a trail of tattered roots and scarred cambium. The same storm felled hundreds of trees across Acadia, and all along the Maine coast and islands. Along the edge of marshes, where salt water seeps inland, spruces are dying, creating a ghostly gray border. The sea, swollen with heat and glacial meltwater, is pushing closer to the trees: a problem still unsolved.

Still, these shores are used to wind and waves, and the boundary between forest and ocean has always been permeable, shifting.

On the beach, biological decay is slow. Dead trees become part of the tideline, protecting the shore from the next storm. Driftwood provides perches for birds; shelter for shrew, mink, and insect; a resting place for wanderers.

Fragments of forest are pulled into the sea with each tide.

Dissolved, forest carbon absorbs light and influences the growth of phytoplankton, the 500-million-year-old ancestors of the trees, the base of the marine food web, producers of much of the oxygen in the atmosphere.

Drifting wood carries seeds and plants to new habitat. Rafts of woody material become floating islands of biodiversity, attracting seabirds and fish and the eggs of the ocean strider, also known as a sea skater or salt treader, the only insect known to live in the open ocean.

Below the surface, organisms like gribbles and shipworms consume cellulose. On the ocean floor, bivalves convert sunken wood, a rare source of energy in the deep sea, to sediment.

The trees have given it all away, their leaves to the insects, their bark to the lichen, their seeds to the birds, their shade to the deer, their roots to the fungi, the rest to the sea and sky.

In exchange, nutrients enter the forest from bones of fish and shells of crab, urchin, and mussel—the feasts of gull, crow, and otter. In autumn, on a high tide, sea-run brook trout may migrate upstream, bringing carbon, nitrogen, and sulfur back into the woods.

Waves crash against the shore, sending salt and other minerals into the air. Wind stirs the surface of the sea, and fog drifts into the trees. As it drips through the canopy to the ground, the cooling mist eases the stress of heat and drought in the coastal forest, where a new generation of trees is growing in the sunlit clearings made by the last storm, and the spruce and fir in their sparkling shade await the next.

THE REVEAL

Carl Little

"The heavy evening fog was caliginous over the harbor."
—Word Daily, sample sentence using "caliginous"

The fog obscures but is not obscure,
moist and real, not cliché soup,
more like consommé. We haven't

the foggiest, except we do, or at least
you can't recall it ever being
this thick, like the wharf scene

in cinema noir, French smugglers
moving booze from the boat,
muffled by the caliginous stuff. Nothing

vague about this fog—we know
its clammy hands, clinging thing
that curls your hair for free and

later completes its thousand veils dance,
moving off to reveal what you've been
desperately looking for and avoiding:

islands and sea, world without end.

AFTER THE SPLASH

Leslie Moore

We step to the porch railing—wine
glasses in hand, Scrabble forgotten—
to spy a bird floundering in the cove,
dashing the sea with great, feathered
downbeats, almost obscured by the spray.
It's a bald eagle and my heart thrashes with it.

I'm ready to canoe to the rescue,
my husband paddling, me leaning
over the bow, poised to pluck a frantic,
flapping, full-grown eagle out of the sea
in my bare arms. Its wingspan is wider
than I am tall, its beak a scimitar.

But the eagle doesn't need me.
It settles onto the water, plump as a duck,
turns beak to shore, scoops the sea with
feathery palms, and climbs out on a rocky
shelf, dragging in one talon a fish,
huge and silvery in sunlight.

FOG TIME

Catherine J.S. Lee

Walk there,
past spruces, through cordgrass,
to the shingle beach where sea-lavender
and glasswort edge the shoreline—
and pause.

Feel the damp coolness
of fog against your summer skin.
Feel the frizzing of your unruly hair.
Feel your restless spirit calm itself—
and breathe.

Listen, actively listen,
as sounds swirl around this salt marsh
through the moist air—
the toll of a bell buoy,
the blast of a lobster boat's horn,
the keening of gulls.

Appreciate this moment
when sight becomes irrelevant
and other senses sharpen—
when the murmur of tidewash intensifies,
and the air holds the weight and substance
of sky-borne clouds brought to earth,
and the flats below the high tide mark
smell sharply of mud and iodine.

Stand within this soft gray cocoon
and wonder at the paradox of fog—
obscuring the obvious
while revealing the subtle,
dense as brick, insubstantial as starlight.

PATCHWORK

Shir Kehila

After dropping my partner off at the Mount Desert Island hospital, I'd go down to walk the shore path. While his blood filled tiny glass vials, mine rushed free through my body, quickened by the views that have so moved me. I usually had just enough time to walk it all the way and back, wishing we'd someday do so together. Even more, I wished he were there now, so I wouldn't have to wish it.

When my partner wasn't around, which was most of the time, other couples were. On the path, I watched teenagers looking out at Egg Rock, a father taking his wife and children's picture, an older man drawing hearts in the sand while his partner filmed, laughing. I smiled while passing her by, but made no eye contact, not wanting to burst the fragile, shimmering bubble of a memory-in-the-making. I committed it to my own, though, adding to an expanding archive of witnessed tenderness. Often, I'd lay its contents on the floor of my mind, as if to collage, then paste a mental insert of my partner inside them, right where I wished he'd go. Wished he *had* been. It was a way to retroactively transport him outdoors: to imagine we too had been seen in passing, within our own shapeshifting bubble. In reality, I was either with him at his parents' home, where we both lived, or I was moving through the world on my own.

The shore path was often full of couples, but it was also full of other things I wished he could see: a silky cloud shawl descending, one blue June day, over a Porcupine island, or seagulls chasing each other one November afternoon through the misty air, a bruised apple in one of their beaks. They took turns dropping it into the waves, then fishing it out like a ball, like kids. I loved watching the path through the seasons, the "same" place made multiple by passing time and weather. It was a special kind of travel: the scenery itself changed—or rather, *was* changing itself—while we stayed put, or kept coming back.

In summer, while the salt breeze was sweetened by beach roses, I wished my partner could put his face to their petals. In fall, I wished he could read the new sign on the old apple tree, politely asking the young to take mercy on its branches. I tried to wrap scenes from the path like pastries, then bring them home to him: the sunset sky in a soft, orange icing, the crescent moon like a silver spoon digging in. But I'd sometimes forget to share these scenes while they were fresh in my mind, then forget about them altogether. They, like most pastries, had a short shelf life.

My partner's blood work, on the other hand, was a long-term routine: a way for his out-of-state doctor to monitor the side effects of his many prescriptions. His parents, brother, and I took turns driving him to the hospital. On the ride back, we'd often pass by a duplex I lived in after college, and my car would struggle up the hill I used to climb on foot, back then, to visit him. I'd go once a week at first, then twice, then every other day, and still never felt ready to leave.

Soon after we started dating, I moved to New York City for grad school. When Covid hit just months later, my partner's parents took me in. I helped out as much as I could, not only to show my gratitude to them, or my love for him, but also to understand, for myself, what he needed: what it'd take for me to meet his needs. I wanted to know whether I could do it. Whether we could live independently, even if he'd still depend on me.

Between chores and Zoom meetings, I scraped by at school, my work on the back burner if not off the stove altogether. Most nights, I moved through the kitchen in a bumpy delirium, cooking meat and grains, veggies and sauce, all four burners turned up to the max to save time. Within months, I broke a glass dish, a ceramic one, and a pepper shaker, and, if this wasn't enough, seared the bottom of a pot into the straw-colored counter. "I'm getting a smoky smell," my partner would sometimes text from upstairs before I noticed any. "If it's charred," I'd sometimes joke, "you know who made it."

As the pandemic eased, and people started traveling again, old college professors and bosses reached out to ask if I'd watch their pets. Pet-sitting was a paying gig that offered what I couldn't afford: a space "of my own," if only borrowed and temporary. I accepted all these offers, having grown sensitive to my position as a guest who—it was starting to seem possible—might never leave. Even if I could become a sole caretaker to my partner, we wouldn't have been able to move out. We didn't have the budget for rent. Not on MDI, not after the pandemic boom, not while only one of us was working. Perhaps not any other way, either. The housing crisis was so severe, it was a question of availability as much as cost, all while—if not *because*—the seasonal vacancy rate kept rising, reaching sixty percent in 2022. It was hard to find a home, it turned out, where most houses stood empty.

And so, my partner and I lived—for now, indefinitely—at his parents'. While their generosity allowed me to stay on the island and, therefore, to stay with their son, pet-sitting offered brief pockets of privacy and a kind of independence I'd almost forgotten. It was a glimpse not only into the life I might have once my partner got better, but also to the one I could have right now, even if nothing else changed. I could spend less time in the kitchen, and yet— or therefore—put my figurative "pot" back on the stove. I could start writing again, using every metaphorical burner, and as few of the real ones as possible. After all, I didn't need the fire alarm going off! Of course, it did anyway.

Soon, I was watching pets for friends-of-friends, then friends-of-friends-of-friends, which was no small privilege. I was honored to be entrusted with both fur people—as I've come to think of pets, per May Sarton's genius—and with the spacious sanctuaries of near-strangers. Whether paint peeled off the walls or shone bright and spotless, the houses were all beautiful to me. Two of those I was often called back to—which couldn't have been more different than one another—overlooked the same bay, their views equally stirring and both changed, in sync, by the same rush and retreat of the tides. From one of them, I watched a seagull fly off with its catch—close enough that I could make out fins—and a row of ducklings parting the morning fog like a curtain. Each home was all windows, not only into other people's lives, or my own, but to the wild and precious ones beyond the glass, and to our shared, ceiling-less home: this coast.

The houses peered back at me, in turn, from the smiling eyes of the owners' loved ones, their faces growing more familiar to me each time I opened the fridge or passed by a framed photo. I grew fond of them, with time, so much so that I recently had to stop myself from approaching someone I recognized in downtown Bar Harbor. I may have seen his pictures, I realized, but he'd never seen me at all.

While my clients took planes across oceans and trains across the country or just drove three hours down the coast, I traveled between their homes, getting in after they'd left and leaving before they'd returned. My calendar was a patchwork of arrivals and departures, an attempt to string multiple short trips into long stretches away from my home base, which wasn't quite my home. Struggling to turn any offer down, I'd often found myself hopping around not just every few days or weeks, but multiple times a day. "Home" became, in my mind, a colorful mix of floors and ceilings, roofs and door-frames, stairs and nightstands—each layered over another in a crazy-quilt-like fashion. Once in a while, I'd find myself searching, in one kitchen, for the contents of another, scouring the counter for an orange Palmolive, say, when a blue Dawn was right in front of me. In place of an address, I'd a lottery-machine-full of them, auto-activated whenever a client texted. Like a hopeful gambler, I watched the numbers—dates of travel—thrown against each other in a mania, desperately willing the new to align with the old.

When dates didn't align, I often forced them to. Overlapping gigs allowed me to extend my wanderings, either by connecting one "patch" to the next or by shortening the gap between them. But I could overdo it, and did. Two winters ago, I spent Christmas taking care of twelve pets in six homes, which meant I spent it on the road between them. As I struggled to keep track of my things—coffee and probiotics on two different counters, Route 102 stretched between them—my partner struggled to keep track of me. "Oh, right!" he'd say, remembering. "You're at so-and-so's tonight!" (So-and-so was usually the pet.) "Yup," I'd reply, "tonight." And we'd laugh. Pet-sitting was easy to joke about because it wasn't always easy to do. It meant constant adjust-ments, and the near-constant fear of damaging things that weren't mine, then packing and unpacking those that were. But, paradoxically, zipping around allowed me to stay close to both my partner and myself. To be near him, but out of his parents' way. Earning too little to rent, my choice wasn't between moving around and staying put, I felt, but between moving around and moving elsewhere.

Whenever I started a gig, one patch clicked into focus against the blurred background of the quilt. For the duration of my stay, "home" was that home, but its features were no longer quite as defined as they'd been at first. When departure drew near, a different patch—my next destination—began obscuring the one I was on. I lived inside the patchwork, placing an insert of myself indoors as I'd done with my partner out on the path. But I never pasted or sewed us. The patchwork was constantly in the making. Never done.

From time to time, on longer gigs, my partner would join me. It was how we first got to experience "our own space" too and how I learned what it would be like to care for him on my own. Thankfully, I didn't have to do it for long. My partner—now husband—started getting better.

When we first walked the shore path together, I kept squeezing his hand, as if to make sure he was there, too excited to be fully present, myself. Another time, we sat on a bench in Grant Park, within sight of Balance Rock. This large boulder, a prominent feature of the path, was transported there by a glacier during the last ice age. Before arriving at its current, perfect tilt, the rock slid down with the ice, as if riding a magic dragon. Movement doesn't only precede or succeed balance, I learned, but makes it possible in the first place. Balance depends—hangs—on movement. Perhaps it's not all that strange, then, that my moves should ground me, or do the same, as I've come to believe they have, for my relationship.

While my partner's blood work remained a monthly fixture of our lives, so did my walks on the shore path. The path itself seemed fixed to me too—sturdy and firm—one of the few places I'd always return to, no matter where "home" happened to be. But the path was not fixed, as last year's storms have shown. Rocks crumbled and washed off, their balances lost. The path became impassable.

Earlier this year, I walked parts of it with a friend on a frigid Sunday afternoon. The frozen snow was slippery, and the path not fully repaired, but we couldn't resist the sweet, pink glaze of the sunset, the call of the water. Arms entwined, my friend and I walked until we reached an area yet to be restored, which we decided to bypass by climbing down to the rocks. I mistook their icy caps for salt and slipped almost instantly. It was a slow-motion fall, and I was luckily unharmed, and somehow less shaken, it seemed, than my friend, who watched helplessly from a different rock. We quickly climbed back up, then dashed off through the trees into private property. We'd seen no one on the path—it was indeed treacherous—and assumed we wouldn't disturb anybody. Within a minute, though, a man appeared as if summoned by a spell.

"You really shouldn't be here," he said.

He had every right to ask us to leave, I knew, and yet, I wanted him to know we were just trying to be safe, that I'd fallen, that it could have been much worse. But something told me he wouldn't have cared. "You should get back on the path," he repeated. The irony, of course, was that there was no path to get back onto. It was the reason we trespassed in the first place. We needed a way around the missing section.

Going around a problem isn't usually an ideal solution. But it may be one in the absence of others. To go around my complicated living arrangement, I've been going all around the island. To keep my balance, I keep moving. I know this is a privilege, available to me only because I do have a place to land—my in-laws'—to patch up the gaps. Because the quilt is a communal one, the work of many hands and paws.

Several months before the path was fully restored, my husband had gone in for his last routine blood work. He's well enough now that it's no longer needed. Last week, I walked the path end to end for the first time in over a year, not as the perk of an errand, but as a pleasure unto itself. I came to enjoy it because it was there again. Because, thanks to the many hands that had patched it up, my eager feet—perhaps like yours—could find their way.

"Mackworth Granite" by Don Peterson

CONTINUUM

Brook Merrow

1

We put in at Churchill Dam and paddled north in our canoe along the Allagash Wilderness Waterway into Umsaskis Lake, which splayed wide, flat, and still. A recent rain left behind a somber sky pressing down upon the water and upon the land, the firs and the spruce.

On the coast in the house by the sea, my mother dozed in a chair, her breath a feathery whisper. She wore an old wool sweater over an old cotton turtleneck, her diminished form lost beneath the shapeless clothing. Afternoon sunlight fell on the beige couch opposite. A fluffy orange cat sprawled on the couch, belly up, in a wash of warmth.

2

Up north the following day, as we traveled across Round Pond, our strength and synchronicity increased. Flexed trapezoids, contracted lumbar muscles. Fully alive, our canoe sprang forward with each stroke. A broad, nameless sky with little interest in the day spread into spaces not claimed. Wind skittered across the water's surface, roughing up row upon row of ripples. Air entered my lungs in huge swoops; only my paddle, dug deep, kept me from lifting away into the sky.

Beneath us, down, down through the depths, lay volcanic and sedimentary rocks, etched with the fine outlines of fossils—brachiopods and gastropods—traces of delicate seashells, remnants of tiny marine invertebrates. All these from hundreds of millions of years ago when a warm tropical sea idled over northern Maine and Canada.

This, while my mother slept on the beige couch not far from the edge of the ocean. The Kindle lay on her stomach, the chapter she selected unread. The cat waited at the sliding glass door, anxious to creep through the garden. My stepfather watched my mother deliberately.

3

On day three under somber skies, we paddled northward, toward Allagash Falls, where we portaged canoes and gear around the exuberant, rocky cataract. Next to our campsite, I swam in the cool, fresh water of the river. As cold as the salt water that lay beyond my mother's house.

At the sea, my mother slept away the summer afternoon in the living room recliner. The tide flowed into the cove, then emptied out. The cat lay curled in her round bed beside the television. My stepfather tried to rouse his wife for dinner, but sleep ran deep. He placed his index and middle fingers on the inside vein of my mother's slight wrist, the pulse regular but faint.

That night on the Allagash, I slept a jagged sleep. I dreamed we were carried downstream in our canoe past tangled alders and cedars; past the conifers and hardwoods; past a single birchbark canoe laid up onshore; past herds of logs, mill-bound, and the craggy old loggers swinging peavey hooks, corralling the timber; past the majestic 150-foot white pines that once stood. In a moment's time, we had surpassed the flow of the Allagash, beating it to the confluence with the St. John River and hurtling along that waterway clear to the open sea. In my dream, the past was new, the present old, the future still older.

4

In the goodness of the morning, below the falls came the sunshine, wiping clean the slate from the sky. Down the grand highway of the river we paddled, through ruffles of whitewater. A boisterous set of rips caught our canoe, turned it sideways against a rock, holding us for an exhilarating moment of sweet danger before releasing us.

At the village of Allagash, we hauled out the canoe and packed up. We drove Route 11 toward Ashland and Bangor, where we would turn southeast to the house on the coast. At the top of a hill in Patten, where we had two bars of cellphone coverage, I learned my mother had passed away early that morning.

Later that day, at the coast, in the quiet of the living room, I looked to the water. I imagined my mother sharing what I observed, and more: a turning tide, the far grumble of diesel-powered lobster boats returning home, cormorants diving beneath the water, gliding like sleek torpedoes. A line of land across the cove, smothered in spruce and pine. And beyond that, all the way to Canada, points and juts and peninsulas and islands, laced with vague dirt roads and rivers and streams, and dotted with white clapboard houses and more fir trees and abandoned granite quarries, and inlets ringed with rocks and seaweed and full to the brim with deep-green salt water.

Like quickened time-lapse footage shot from above, the miles below swept by us in rapid succession northward and eastward, until the geographic features were all used up and all that remained were clouds that part and repart, a sun that rises and sets again, and a moon that shapes and reshapes and eclipses time after time.

COFFINS NECK COVE

Susan Doyle

He carried the sea in his heart.
She, the forest.

Surf and salt mingled with earth and pine
The vast blue and the deep green
For just a tide's time.
Each then, went separate ways.

The memory of a once union
In the reflection of shore.

A SHOAL

Richard Foerster

Stenotomus chrysops

At the river's mouth, a shoreward surge
of porgies spilled from the surf

where the tide roiled with bluefish
and harbor seals schooled in ferocities

of hunger. They slashed the mercuric
flanks of their prey till the air blazed

like shattered mirrors under the angling
sun. We stood on the rocks awhile, safe

in our astonishment, and watched
the sea contuse with the blood of thousands.

Soon there was nothing more to keep us
from the darkened path toward home,

except for the brief flash of the headland within
its gathering sweep, its blind, imperious gaze.

TOTAL ECLIPSE

Betty Culley

When the sisters tell how fast
the air and sand turned
cold, and the sudden
darkness,

there's still wonder
in their voices remembering
the two little girls
they were,
shivering
on the disappeared beach,

maybe partly aware even then
that this moment would repeat
itself over and over
in future stories
and in the shared spaces
of their childhood minds.

WE HAD A HOME ON MDI

Melodie Prescott Greene

"I had a farm in Africa" ... no, no, no. That's Isak Dinesen's line, not mine; although she too was elderly—in the movie, at least—when she wrote her memories back to life. Which can be easier said than done, sometimes, when the memories are fifty years old. Let's start again.

I had a home on MDI. Actually, Tony and I had a home on MDI, *L'Isle des Monts-desert* as the early French explorers and mapmakers called it. I was thinking of Tony today, that earthy-Capricorn lover of mountains and music and seas, with whom I'd hiked so many island trails and climbed so many of those beautiful, barren heights that Samuel de Champlain saw in 1604. Mostly housebound now, Tony lives in a condo south of here, our married life far behind us. Or should I say "in us"? Because, in memory, whatever *was* still *is*, however nebulous the border between life events and the traces they leave, that can shift and settle and settle and shift from one recollected version to the (recollected) next.

In our early twenties, Tony and I could ill afford a summer rental, so we pitched a tent near our hippie friends'—it was the early seventies—on Nelse Herrick's scrubby backland. That first summer, we had a litter of Bangor-born kittens to care for—the next summer, a baby not yet three months old. The only water we glimpsed around Herrick's dry scrub was in jugs we'd filled and brought in ourselves. But each early fall, when the tourists had gone, we folded our tent and moved to a sweet, little cottage we'd found—at a reasonable, off-season rate—overlooking the bay from behind a widely curving seawall made of countless granite boulders trimmed with strands of dried-brown seaweed and lavender-and-light-green urchin shells that had long since lost their spines; and broken bits of fishing gear and paper-light crab carcasses; and silvery-weathered driftwood shapes; and feathers, sticks, and mollusk shells. The seawall both separated and joined the land and the sea, the here and the there, the then and the now, as the giving-taking twice-a-day tides transformed it from one shifting, settling structure to the (shifting, settling) next.

Memories can be consciously called to mind (recalled) or recollected, which must be what happened when I pictured our place on MDI today. As science would have it, thoughts of Tony excited nearby neurons connected to other items in the "Tony-and-me" collection. *Et voila!* There was the cottage, the seawall, the black-and-white photo that Rick took of Tony and our curly-haired toddler—the one sitting in the guitar case—laughing their heads off! I can hear them now, I swear. And now I see the happy puppy that bounded into our lives with her Collie-mix colors and bushy-waggy tail, her big-hearted smile, and her sweet, sweet way of "oofing" back when spoken to that made you think she must surely be in on the joke. She loved hiking too. As did baby in her backpack.

Sometimes, remembering is more like guessing your way through a fog that has snuck silently in on those "little cat feet," blurring boundaries and people and time. In the distance, a fog bank looks like a solid gray wall, an opaque force of nature with a will of its own (it seems). It's only after you've breached the fog's trompe l'oeil wall, like Alice through the looking glass, and experienced the surreal reality of its passive, formless, vanishing-Cheshire-cat ways that you might see something that's not fog, even if you don't yet know what it is … or where a sound is really coming from … or how close the next something might be. Memory can be like that.

I can't recall hearing fog horns at the cottage, but they echo through the soundtrack of the first half of my life, and the several grown-up water babies I knew then. Cancers all—cardinal water, sign of the crab, ruled by the moon— they were never happier than when skittering across some beach somewhere or sailing the mothering sea in shells of their own with the people they loved. We saw seagulls play tag in the blue-sky salt breeze, and heard horns, bells, and lapping waves in the wet-gray-mist fogs; we knew green was for starboard and red was for port and that "red right returning" meant heading for home.

At low tide, live crabs and other creatures—still wearing their shells—appeared on the uncovered beach at the foot of the seawall, with limpets, snails, and whelks sitting *on* the beach while the clams remained *in* it (their air holes a dead giveaway, sometimes literally). And tidal pools—little niche kingdoms all their own—where depressions in the bedrock-trapped seawater and the life it held, with near-translucent, tiny crabs and tiny, shrimp-shaped swimmers the largest animals you could actually see. We might find smoothly sanded, colored glass—cobalt blue the best—or occasional, scratch-your-head oddities, like the London police whistle I picked up one day that had "THE Metropolitan" stamped on its shiny-metal side. I'd rather not think about what went on beneath the slimy, gold-green seaweed, except to say that the close-knit colonies of barnacled, blue-shelled mussels pretty much called it home.

Skittering crabs had the run of the beach; they moved much faster than the shell-bound crew. All legs—the only parts you could usually see—hermit crabs had shells too, but that was scavenged housing, easy to abandon when they were ready to trade up. Hermits rarely skittered since they hauled their heavy homes. And horseshoe crabs didn't skitter at all. Nor did they look much like crabs. Or horseshoes, for that matter. Neither crabs nor crustaceans, it turns out they're arachnids, like their spider and scorpion kin. Often called "living fossils," apparently—they haven't changed much in 250 million years—horseshoe crabs look like World War II German helmets with long, spiky tails. Did I mention they're related to scorpions?

I've combed many a low-tide beach in my life, and there's only one where I ever saw horseshoe crabs. I was young at the time, and they were shockingly big compared to the other crabs I'd seen. Somewhat shocking too were the ancient relatives we visited there, at their summer cottage. (Old people seemed a lot older then, like living fossils themselves. Imagine what memories *they* recollected.) Most shocking of all was their outdoor toilet—"the outhouse," the old-timers called it: a creaky, bridge-like walkway, built on crazy-skinny poles, that extended out over the water and must have been fifteen feet above it by the time you reached the business end. And not an environmental law in sight! Creaky, scary walkway ... crazy-skinny poles ... waves moving back and forth beneath the hole (!) I sat on (with a definite breeze up my butt) ... alligators, I mean, fossils all around ... and shockingly scary-big counterfeit crabs ... some things are hard to forget.

Our cottage, Tony's and mine, was near a narrow isthmus that joined the mainland to a point—nearly an island—that jutted a few miles into the open ocean. One time, after staying up all night with friends, we went outside at first light and, from the top of the seawall, saw the full moon setting on one side of the isthmus and the sun rising on the other. The pastel-beautiful, brightening sky was what my oldest friend used to call sky-blue-pink. (I want to add Venus to that glorious sky—to herald the rising sun—but I fear I'd be making it up.) We often walked to the end of the point and back just to move in the great outdoors, and see it and feel it and smell it and hear it. We were magnificent beasts back then, amid nature's finest fauna—in the woods, in the water, in the sky, on the shore—and her wonderful flora, of course (of course)—scented cedar and beach rose and pine; wild cranberries for Thanksgiving sauce; the circles of alders and tall, pointed firs; red berries in winter, pussy willows in spring ... in the most beloved Eden on earth (on earth).

World War II General George Patton said, "The fog of war works both ways. The enemy is as much in the dark as you are." We magnificent beasts—the ones with the big brains—have long been working on ways to not have to fight each other for survival. It's not going well. The movie *Out of Africa* portrays, in part, how Danish-born Karen Blixen—the woman behind her Isak Dinesen pen-name—and her mostly English friends dealt with World War I in far-east Africa. We had a war in my time too: Vietnam. It ended on April 30, 1975. A week or two later, Tony and I hosted an end-of-the-war celebration at our home on MDI.

I can't recall much about that day, I'm afraid; in fact, the only person, besides me, that I'm certain was there was Tony. But there's one foggy memory of me standing in front of the long kitchen counter—which was covered with food—greeting folks who were dropping off or picking up food, or making their way to or from the bathroom. Less foggy, but briefer, is the image of the many friends and friends of friends spread out, side by side, on the beach that night, each holding a lit candle. If Tony got us singing, I don't know what we sang (although John Lennon's "Imagine" would have been perfect). But, with the world's connected oceans touching all its disparate lands, I like to imagine that some of the ripples reflecting our candlelight that night touched beautiful Cam Ranh Bay.

I want to add a full moon (more illumination! more reflection!) to that moth-eaten, Cheshire-cat memory of mine—not much left but the smile—but I think I'd be making that up too. As my younger self said on page one, writing memories back to life can be easier said than done, sometimes, when the memories are fifty years old. Let's start again.

SALT DAWN

Patricia Smith Ranzoni

          Fogged in
on Bailey off Orrs off the main.
Only morning stars are blurs
by restaurant, stores, motels,
and (the world's only) cribstone bridge. So thick
it drains like rain off leaves. Lobster-
boat motors float unseen like tractors
in neighboring fields back home. Fishing families hollering from docks that's
what's being lost: work calling for shouts.
Not the demeaning master-over-owned
kind but earnest teaching talk
from urgent hard work
no pussyfooting around.
Orders to avoid catastrophe
grounded on respect,
on being there together
against all odds.

          Barefoot
on sopping sod, on gravel
and sand (island crumbs)
to ledge where lichen and Queen
Anne's lace dress land's end.
Adirondack slats wet,

chamois shirt a sponge. Gulls
make her miss her rooster's inland
yell but give an altogether equally
fine crow to incoming light. Some, alarm-
ing, like hens when something's
weasled into their eggs. All fowl (coastal
or farm) go *oh! oh!* The necessary calls.
The voices raised for death and life and
territorial integrity. From across tidal pools:
creature screeches and throaty whines
and squawks exactly like socket tensions
from pleading-their-need-for-grease
working wheels.

> *There they go*
throwing tide like snowplows
before most folks are up. Over to Mackerel Cove
looking for all the world like the fish itself, wakes
ripple the water's surface, a slippery skin
to the ocean's muscle. Wooden pencil sticky.
Silences of bird-oil on pinfeathers.
Overhead glide. Dew jeweled chamomile,
black-eyed-Susans, seaweed, shells. The music
water makes waded in, pecked through, lifted off.
Her tablet dampens, softens toward pulp.
Back to its treeness its first nature.
Exposed trunks of shore stone could be mammoth
trees downed eons ago, ancient grains raised in their own
long return. Deadly nightshade defies from rock
pockets, dangling purple and yellow candle charms
fruiting to seagreen pearls on the way to *stop* red.

> *What roots here*
> *holds to heaven*
> *and fights like hell!*

Her nightdress hem
is soaked, her hair.
She resents even her glasses
coming between her self
and her source.
Takes them off
to feel full face
what she needs to see close.
Nostrils and lungs
and tongue saturated
with origin.

SANDALWOOD

Amanda Neitz

Knock three times and enter
Cross the threshold between now and then
That pulsing ancient metronome
Pulls the drumbeat in.

Standing silent in the circle
Shell and feather, stone and moss
I have loved a thousand oceans
Carrying ancient worlds across

Draw down the sacred light
I will swallow moons
A shipmate of Ulysses
Hurricanes to salt-swept dunes

Undulating grasp on forever
Sway to rhythms from the tide
Shell and feather, stone and moss
Wave and rock both coincide

Carry my driftwood body
Along the coastline of my heart
Let the sun try to break me
And return my silence to the earth

THE EXTINCTION OF *AMMOSPIZA CAUDACUTA*

Matt Bernier

They will leave like lovers,
these saltmarsh sparrows
fluttering toward extinction,

sea level rise lifting all boats
but not these cupped nests
with four speckled eggs,

king tides marching armies
toward helpless hatchlings
crying like Moses in a basket,

and even the male's polygamy
will not outrun climate change,
orangey eyebrows and mustaches

lusting the streaking of females,
white bellies in soft surrender,
perched upon grass hummocks

their flight songs unspooling
like sacred music about exodus,
notes gurgling like parting seas.

"The Swim" by Nancy Dewey

THE SALTWATER CURE

Andrea Lani

It's the first week of April, and I feel an overwhelming urge to hear the sound of ocean waves and look out over an endless expanse of blue water. For decades, I was a strictly seasonal shore-goer, digging my toes in the sand only in the heat of summer, but for the past couple of years I've made a point of going to the beach at least once every month and have come to love the shifting mood of the ocean in all seasons. But it's been a cold winter, heavy with dark political realities and losses closer to home, and I haven't visited the ocean since the last day of December when my husband, our oldest son, and I made our way to the nearest beach and dove into the water.

This is something my friends and I used to do in college, before "cold plunging" was a household term: jump off the dock behind campus or pick our way through ice blocks and wade into the waves rolling onto the shore at Ship Harbor. But as I got older, I became a wimp about cold water, and I hadn't immersed myself in the Gulf of Maine outside of the July-to-September "warm" season in nearly thirty years. But New Year's Eve was an unusually balmy day, and I'd just read Katherine May's *Wintering*, in which she extolls the physical and mental benefits of winter sea swims. It was also a week after my mother-in-law died unexpectedly on Christmas Day, and I felt both the need to escape the oppressive atmosphere of a house in mourning and to experience the healing power of salt water. I thought it would be good for my husband and son as well—our other two children being away with friends that day—and so I coaxed them into joining me as I ran screaming through the shallows until I reached water deep enough to dive under.

The sea was not much colder on that December day than it is in August, and when I emerged from the water, my skin tingled all over, my head felt clearer than it had all week, and I was infused with an energy I hadn't experienced in months. I remembered other times that a swim in the ocean had abated some heartache or other, as well as the famous Isak Dinesen quote: "I know a cure for everything: Salt water—sweat, or tears, or the salt sea." I half-planned to make it a regular practice—weekly or monthly swims in the ocean. But on January 1, winter settled in and didn't let up for four months. It's now April, and it snowed last week and is forecast to snow again next week. Today's not even that warm—mid-forties and windy—but cabin fever has struck and I need to get out. The sea is calling to me.

I have no intention of taking a plunge into the water, however. Whatever madness put it into my head that I'd make that a routine has long since passed. Instead, I pack a cookie and a water bottle, a notebook and a pen, dress in layers, and head to a nature preserve about an hour from my house. Once there, I wind my way through a forest of tall spruce and oak trees along a mile and a half or so of soft duff interrupted by boardwalks that cross wetlands teeming with the red spathes of skunk cabbage, spring's first flower. From the final rise of land, the ocean comes into view through the trees, a vast blue expanse that appears almost like a wall, a flat-topped mountain range. It is a place where one world collides with another.

I caught my first impression of the Atlantic Ocean early on an August morning thirty-two years ago. I'd just completed the next-to-last leg of a 2,200-mile cross-country Greyhound bus trip, arriving at Boston's South Station at 3 a.m., with three hours to wait before my final bus would arrive. Outside the station, the air was filled with a briny smell that I was certain meant the sea was nearby, and I would have wandered off in search of it if it weren't for the enormous duffel bag—all of the possessions I'd need for the next three months—crouching at my feet. So instead, I waited on a bench outside the station, breathing in deep the salt air and listening to the hew and cry of gulls as the sky lightened toward daybreak. From the window of the bus to Maine, I peered out to the east, catching glimpses of sparkling blue water whenever the highway came within viewing distance of the coast, but I wouldn't truly experience the ocean with all of my senses until several hours later when I finally arrived in Bar Harbor, at the campus of College of the Atlantic on the shore of Frenchman Bay.

The trail descends the hill and makes a sharp right turn, bordering the coast for a half mile or so. Here, the oak and spruce forest gives way to a rocky ledge that slopes down toward the water. Near the top, the stone is dark gray quartzite, wavy from the pressures of metamorphosis and threaded with thin seams of white quartz. Below that is a band of pinkish-white granite, intruded with wide strips of quartz, and below that, the rock is stained rusty red with a slick green coating of algae. The rocks of the lowest tier are invisible, draped in army-green seaweed.

The ocean is restless today, bluish-gray, choppy with whitecaps and waves that hiss and sigh when they break against the shore. The blue sky is striped with bands of thin, gauzy cirrus clouds, and a steady wind blows. I sit down on the uppermost ledge, trying to position myself so that I'm both in the sun and out of the wind with a wide-open view of the sea. A solitary loon rests on the water a few dozen yards from shore, a gull flies close to the ocean's surface to my left, and a raft of eiders, four black-and-white males and five brownish females, drifts close to the headland to my right.

I spent my first week in Maine as part of a flotilla of red and yellow sea kayaks, traveling from island to island with a group of fellow students and an instructor. We cooked our meals of spaghetti or couscous over campfires, slept beneath the stars or in the fog, and dove into the cold ocean daily, the water leaving behind a salty white bloom on our skin and rendering our hair as coarse as straw. Before we embarked on our trip, we spent an afternoon learning to wet exit a capsized boat. We flipped ourselves over in our kayaks, pulled our spray skirts off the coaming, and slipped out of the boat, which we then righted and clambered back on board to do it again.

Before that day, hanging upside down from my kayak in the dark water of the cove behind the college, I'd only ever immersed myself in water that was clear, chlorinated, and contained within a concrete pool. I knew almost nothing about the ocean, despite a teenage fascination with cetaceans, which manifested in the acquisition, during my freshman year in college, of an ankle tattoo of two dolphins swimming in a circle (the tattoo, which was copied from a graphic in *The Greenpeace Book of Dolphins* and cost $15 at Lurch's Fine Dermagraphics in Dallas, Texas, is often mistaken for a pair of blue lips; I'm lucky it didn't give me hepatitis). I'd lived my whole life far inland—eighteen years in Colorado and three semesters at a university in Texas—and I'd only come into contact with the sea once before, on a family trip to the Pacific coast when I was ten years old. There, I'd waded into the gray water lapping an Oregon beach only as deep as my ankles, thanks to the early spring chill and my mother's horror of "the undertow," which she spoke of as if it were a sentient being lurking offshore, ready to snatch little girls off the sand and drag them into the ocean's depths.

"The edge of the sea is a strange and beautiful place" begins the second of Rachel Carson's sea trilogy books. On that sea kayak trip, I immersed myself in this strange beauty. Everything I encountered was new and enchanting. I learned that there were no *sea*gulls, but got to know herring gulls, great black-backed gulls, and, my favorite, laughing gulls, with their sleek black heads and ironic white-rimmed eyes. I learned to differentiate these gulls from the osprey that also glided overhead and sometimes dropped from the sky, splashed into the water, and emerged clutching fish in their talons. I crouched beside tide pools, studying the dog whelks and periwinkles, sea urchins and sea stars, hermit crabs and blue mussels. I watched barnacles open their front doors and stick out their tongue-like legs with which they scooped microscopic plankton from the water. I slipped and slid over rocks matted with bladder wrack and rockweed and marveled over huge stalks of kelp and sea colander that had let go of their holdfasts and washed up on shore. I saw harbor seals pop their heads up and watch us paddle past, and I repeatedly mistook lobster buoys for seal heads.

I arrived in Maine a week after my twentieth birthday. For much of the previous decade, I'd cultivated an air of teenage eye-rolling ennui and cynicism. The only sincere emotions I allowed myself to express were indignation and outrage, and my growing awareness of politics, environmental destruction, and patriarchy gave me plenty to be outraged about. It had been years since I'd indulged in wonder, joy, or, god forbid, delight. Like the creatures of the intertidal zone, I'd grown a hard outer shell to protect myself from the harsh and dangerous world. But there, on the coast of Maine, I began to shed the carapace that had inured me to magic. I was thousands of miles away from those whose disapprobation and mockery I feared. The novelty of this place where the tide washed in and out on a regular, but continually shifting, schedule, and the animals were shaped like rocks, or stars, or pincushions, woke up my dormant sense of wonder, and that dunking under the cold water of the cove on my first day in Maine was a baptism of a sorts, a rebirth in nature, the salt water dissolving my armor. In crossing the threshold from land to sea, I too transitioned from a hard and resistant way of being into a softer and more tender and open one.

After a while, my sunny spot on the rock slips into shade, and I grow stiff and chilled sitting in the onshore breeze, so I rise to my feet and continue down the path paralleling the coast. The trail crosses a small stream that tumbles down through a break in the rocky shoreline and feeds into the cove amid a boulder-strewn depression that is generously labeled "Cobble Beach" on the preserve map. I remember once when I was in college walking on the shore near campus and coming upon a thin, clear stream of water flowing into the sea. The fellow student I was with told me that, in places where fresh water meets salt water, negative ions are generated, and these in turn create feelings of well-being—although he probably said "good vibes." I've never tried to verify either the chemical or psychological accuracy of this statement, and I've grown more skeptical of new-agey notions of wellness over the years. Nevertheless, I stand on the plank bridge over the stream and imagine good vibes ions fizzing through the air and popping in happy little bursts in my brain. It's not quite as invigorating as a plunge into cold water, but it does feel good.

On the last day of my inaugural sea kayak trip, the sky was clear blue and the seas calm. We had all day and not far to go, so we took our time paddling the final stretch toward campus. As we were crossing a channel between islands, someone pointed their paddle toward the open sea. A pair of harbor porpoises—mother and baby—were swimming toward us, their bodies cresting the surface and dipping below the water in perfect synchrony. I rested my paddle across my spray skirt and watched their paired dorsal fins arc in and out of the water, mesmerized. Despite my tattoo, I'd never seen a dolphin in real life. They came closer and closer, their path directly in line with the port side of my boat. Their smooth gray backs crested one last time and dove beneath the water, perhaps ten or fifteen feet from my kayak. I watched their sleek bodies, one large and one small, slip effortlessly through the shimmering dark water, as they passed beneath my boat and reemerged on the other side, again cresting the surface ten or fifteen feet away. I watched them continue on their way, cresting and diving, cresting and diving, until they vanished into the blue swells. Then I picked up my paddle, dipped it in the water, and made my way toward my new home.

MOON SPINNER

Andrea Suarez Hill

From the river's bed
    a moon sated and
silver crawls over the flats,
    meets lead-red mud,
moves my horizon,
    reshapes the shore,
unseats mauve skies and
    slate grey clouds
above a drain tide
    as a poem lets loose
with a pull words work
    on gravity channeled
through an inner sea.

WANDERING SEARS ISLAND AT DAYBREAK

Cynthia Reeves

"Until everything was rainbow, rainbow, rainbow!"
—Elizabeth Bishop, "The Fish"

1.
The slate-gray sea's swell and ebb
move carelessly through time.
Fish leap into golden cataracts of light
as rocks smoothed to pebbles
count the years of the primeval
water's course. One trail leads inland
to an unremembered dwelling,
fieldstone footing rooting
among towering evergreens
and thorny raspberry vines,
a carpet of bluebells and olive moss
interleaving the crumbling foundation.
All is silence now but
imagine not long ago, red chairs framing
a table set with a half-finished puzzle—
birds, branches, nest emerging—abandoned
by a long-forgotten husband
guiding his wife through a do-si-do.
Imagine the father stretching his bow
to test its tensile strength
before hunting the white-tailed doe

vanished through the hedgerow—
food to tide his brood overwinter.
Imagine the mother stirring
the morning oats as they thicken
in a cast-iron pot cradled
by flames blackening the hearth.
Imagine their children at this same table,
forks suspended over the last
of Sunday ham and roast potatoes
to watch the dance of their parents' years.
Imagine these dreams of home
tucked safely in their memory.

2.
A single, brown-stippled falcon
catches the wind just right,
hang-glides down to perch
on relics of the home's far wall,
eyes the muddy creek for prey,
spies a gold-breasted kingfisher
guarding a nest of gloss-white eggs.
Half-eaten minnows and sticklebacks
dangling from his beak, the father
feeds the one fledgling curious enough
to have broken through its shell.
The falcon waits patiently, waits
for that inevitable instant of carelessness,
snatches the nestling in its claws,
rises into blue, doesn't let go.

3.
Let go.
This sea, this home, these trails
count the days between lifetimes.
Paths lead nowhere and everywhere.

My father knew these things.
That's why he told me,
Before you leave home,
take this map and trace its winding ways
until you know them by heart.
And just for luck, here's my heart.
Keep it with you. You'll need it,
just as you needed that yellow waterproof
your mother pressed into your hands
to ward off the unpredictable.
As if everything could be foreseen,
even the clearing of a morning's
hazy gray to gilded streams of light,
to sun and sudden rainbow.

STORM PREP

Gary Rainford

Freezing fog tonight. South winds, forty to fifty knots
with gusts up to sixty, and sixteen-foot seas. Walking after
supper, a yellow speck finds my headlamp when I scan

the side of the road. I bend down. I scoop out a statue
of snow with my glove and find a small metal cross with
the Serenity Prayer etched into it, a petition to God

for peace and strength. I stuff the icon in my pocket until
I get home. Then I lean it against a bottle of virgin olive oil
on the kitchen counter. Filling water bottles and a stock

pot in case the island loses power, *God grant me wisdom,*
God grant me wisdom, God grant me wisdom, loops in my head.
When my mother remarried, my stepfather—recently sober—

hung a Serenity Prayer wall decoration behind the back
door with my mother's collection of souvenir spoons and
knick-knacks. I look out the window when I hear a thumping

crash. The plastic sled I use to lug firewood summersaults
across the dooryard. Courage, I conclude after a lifetime of
mistakes, is a gale warning, a stillness.

ON THE EDGE

Annaliese Jakimides

I've been driving more than an hour each day to the ocean for weeks now. Although our tidal shoreline is the fourth-longest in the country, holder of first light, this coast is undramatic, a beach that even at the height of beach weather only sports a dot of a human here and there. A quiet rage shifting under the swell of its lip, the ocean exposes its nubby stone carpet of deserted winter.

I leave my apartment early enough to be waterside by the time the cone of new light jostles on the horizon. I'm surprised at how easily my eyes adjust to this version of reality. Well, no, not just the eyes.

We begin in water.

Born of a wild wind, come, it seems, to test whether it's true.

Stunned into submission, taste buds juggle salt and grit. Last night, I was dreaming of the sea that erupts in the month that comes after—after all the others, all the others we know.

Somewhere, I've the words to keep everything alive.

Lines blur as the state of shifting worlds comes now to feel natural to me.

This morning, when I left my small inland city, the wind was stiff, the temperature was twenty-seven, the sky was dark except for the tint of streetlights. Wool jacket, headband, gloves, and, just in case, a pair of red-and-yellow handknit mittens like I used to make every winter up north. My youngest lost so many single mittens, despite the strings and buttons and safety pins, that he learned to knit replacements—and with his begrudgingly acquired new skill, then for years made capes for his little plastic men.

In that world, I always wore mittens, sometimes double—warm, safe, more sensible, fingers nestled next to each other, blood flowing.

On the back seat of the car, I leave an old woolen blanket—witness to child after child, a sleep on the couch by the woodstove, perhaps a living room tent—so that I can be here early enough to watch night become day, dark become light, wrapped in a shroud of beloved stories.

This morning's sheet of fog rolls in over the water. Water that has slapped all kinds of shores far beyond mine, water that has evaporated in one place, traveled across the sky in clouds, and fallen in another land, this land. I taste the otherness on my lips. And I wait.

My face turned up into the early light that lies on the back of this sea, I hear a slight whistle, a human whistle, but no human is in sight. I wonder whether someone will finally walk down the beach. To this place I come, this place where reality seems not quite as certain of itself, where the invisible makes sense, where stories with multiple endings or multiple middles or multiple beginnings are welcome.

Dreams fragment.

The carpet fractures, and something new—well, unanticipated—encounters the possibility of revelation.

I hear another whistle down the beach.

My youngest learned how to whistle from a clarinetist I brought to our small, rural school to show them a jazz musician in action—to show my children and all the others, many of whom in all their lives will never leave these towns that open north, toward the Allagash, Katahdin land. I'm not sure what I was showing them, except that the world is big and options are unlimited, even though what they saw was small and what they heard was country music.

I've been gone from that land for a long time. My son from all land.

I can't locate this whistling. Maybe it's a few yards back from the wild rugosa rose bushes, all scruffy and wind-blown. I can't be sure. My sense of direction has never been good, but now it's downright useless. And none of it matters. Nothing matters except that I'll be here tomorrow and the next day and the next, abraded a bit, rubbed raw in places, burnished to an exquisite sheen in others.

Whenever I think of this son and water, first I think of how he would go forever without a shower if no one paid attention, and then take one only once I insisted. But that's what I think of—my head reaction, the cerebral observation. But when I see him—when the vision of him by water comes unbidden—he is always standing on the edge of Vinalhaven Quarry, his toes curled over the rough rock edge, about to relinquish all that holds him to the earth—although I only saw him standing there, at the quarry, in that spot, in that way, just one summer afternoon. One golden summer afternoon when we'd come to hear the jazz whistler play in his world.

Neither of us ever saw a quarry again.

When you live in Maine, people immediately think of the coast, the ocean, but that's not our world. We're inland people. River people. Our boundaries are forest and rock. The way seeds fall and grow into trees, are then culled, cut out from their roots, taken away and transformed into something else, like tables or bowls, flooring, paper. Rocks are gathered from the fields, not so much to build walls as to make the ground tillable, and walls are the easiest way to handle huge rocks buried in the earth.

Our world was sturdy, solid—or so it seemed.

With the ocean, you walk off the ground, lose your footing and must figure out another way to continue moving. Another way to continue being human.

This boy of mine was not a water boy, a boat boy, a beach boy. But, oh, he was indeed a swift-as-a-swallow, elegant-armed swimmer. I never learned how to swim, a city kid walking to the point at Malibu—not the California one, but the Boston one hidden in the shadow of a subway line. The Red Cross tried to teach about forty of us one summer, but all I remember is lying with my legs beached on the hot sand, belly-down, my face in the shallows, trying to accept the salty waves banging against it.

I wasn't successful. All I can do is float and not well or for long, and so I took my kids to our little spit of a public beach in the north by a pond, fresh water—no salt or waves, resistance—not just to hang out and play, splash around, but also for the two weeks of swimming lessons the town provided so all our children wouldn't drown.

Day after day, here I stand where land slips away under the rippling surface, an otherness of possibilities.

There is nothing against which to measure this coming and going, the shifts, the wind on my face, only a sea of sweet nothingness. I am blind to this place beyond the beyond, behind the scrim of the horizon, the weak, translucent light, the buoy bouncing on the lip of a mid-swell wave, crab shells amid burbles of pink and silver sparkle in the sand, the fluorescent green kayak out in the deep.

Day after day, here I am.

I am here.

Until.

One day, I spread my arms and spin around, or as much as I can spin with winter boots on, digging tiny, centripetal canyons of cold sand along the beach with its lapping waters and the whistling, a composition of sounds that have no identifiable connection, just a transcription of breath from inside and outside, from the land on which I stand, from the sky, from the branches of the leafless rosebushes, from the distant waves that rock the distant kayak, from everything and everywhere.

I open my mouth. A kind of song floats out until my lips close, and a whistle stutters itself into the air all around me.

THIS LIFE

Betty Culley

As time passes,
and it gets harder and easier
to think of
leaving this life,
when the beauty and the ugliness
deepen in ways that shred your heart,
go to the place where the sand
meets the sea,
where unstoppable waves
are like a second steady heartbeat,
and look out
the way so many humans before you
have done, to where the water
blurs into the distant sky,
until it feels possible again.

"Sea Ice, Maquoit Bay, March 2025" by Karen Egee

PORT CLYDE: SEPTEMBER 2023

Cynthia Reeves

Nothing but pilings remain, footprint of the old cannery
where once conveyors throbbed, sardines cartwheeled

as if they could swim backward. Scales glazed, blades
flashed, eyes flung open even as heads fell into waste.

Fish crammed four by four and shut away in tins
coursed the line. A hiss rose, the giant steamer streamed

fog from broken seals. Canning women chattered
to factory rhythms, metal-on-metal shriek of gears,

rollers, drums—oh, the noise!—passing their lives on.
My grandmother toiled on this ship, sixty years,

the twelve-hour shift, a continuous flow of fish. It seemed
to carry her someplace. The general store where she bought

her nickel coffee gone, too, to fire and heartbreak.
Once upon a time, battered tools—threadbare wrench,

tattered hammer, a rusty lock lamenting its forgotten key—
hung preserved in a timber frame above the counter. Steam

spiraled above glass pots, and the wooden flooring gleamed
then darkened, unburdening time. Standing on the pier,

my back to black and ash shrouded in evening mist,
I imagine the thrum of industry, women's laughter,

and that brass bell above the general store's door tolling,
while faraway keening of the Monhegan Ferry fades into dusk.

FOG: HAIKU

Catherine J.S. Lee

one gull calls
    and then another ...
    morning fog

fog-bound cove
the sudden rise
of a great egret

dissolving fog
silhouettes of sunlit geese
graze the meadow

tendrils of fog
old rowboat abandoned
to lupine

summer night
a freighter's horn lengthens
through the fog

SUMMER VISITORS, BUCKSPORT

Kathleen Ellis

Visitors enter the house and take in everything
as though it were their own; they have fled

their other lives. I watch the knowing winks
between them, lighted nuns in hallways.

The Eastern Channel's a midnight rendezvous,
or a jagged hole in the aging deer fence

where marauders have broken through the wire,
but no one (not the coast guard nor the guests

who have finally gone to bed) is stopping them.
Shrouded in low-lying fog, I watch the swirling eddies

of stars drift over the compost heap, and though it's too soon
in the year for night-hawks, a night-hawk calls out

its sharp notes over the bay.

SOUTH SIDE OF HASKELL'S, EARLY SPRING

Kara Douglas

If I close my eyes and breathe, I can feel them still,
the swells that nudge us, nudge us
as we nose down the west side of Haskell's Island,
first sunny break in weeks, it seems.

We watch waves flood against the windward shore,
ink-dark ocean transformed into foaming spray.
Fractals of sky vanish and reform on the water's skin all around us,
two paddlers in a vast sea.

Beneath us, sea rise,
her fury racing at the shore,
her mercy, reaching to submerge everything,
to gather islands like this in her primordial embrace.

On the surface, we feel the lift and fall of her body, moving
sideways
like a snake,
like a lullaby, as we round toward the south point,
exposed,
cradled only by the thin shells of kayaks,
propelled by something as old and unfathomable as these waters.

The swells steepen and come faster, now,
exposing those parts of ourselves we only call forth
in moments like these,
when holding the course isn't enough,
when each stroke is made in response to a greater whole,
a fleeting moment,
a coming to be,
a choosing for something again and again.

The wind lifts a little as we round the point and turn east,
where the water lays down and the sky grays to silver.
Vertical ledges crowned with spruce
stand like sentinels above the water line.
You glance back once and then we stroke again,
silently
toward the unfolding.

IN ACTUALITY, THE OCEAN

Erin Covey-Smith

It's cricket season but there aren't any crickets yet,
falling out of their "supposed to" time like everything
this summer—a busted pocket of jacks.

There is plenty of worry, which crickets like to gnaw,
sawing their sad songs with it.

What we have instead is the ocean so close you can taste it,
its salt scented by wildflowers as it mists its way up
from the shoreline.

Wildflowers which are, inexplicably, on time,
singing of sun while living in fog.

When nothing is always anymore, in actuality, the ocean
is where it always is—but also has given itself over to air,
to scent, to all-encompassing embrace.

We have so much to learn.

UNCERTAINTY

faith lane

i love foggy days
sea smoke
or pea soup
mysteries abound

inside my head, though ...
fog of uncertainty
renders me motionless
unknown dangers lying in wait
who
what
from whence
all shrouded in mist
lurking

WHITEHEAD CLIFF REVISITED

Kate Kearns

This epic expanse, this height, the lungs are too small for it—
the sea a vast, deep green gone velveteen in the gust. Light
lands on the sea like first snow as if you could walk to its edge.
Beach rose stalks, stripped to thorns and crimson hips,

brown from a dry summer, stick up unlovely between
abundant asters, pale purple sunsets. Far below, too far,
a clutch of long black birds cluster at the rocks. Cormorants,
from the way they hang their wings to dry. A vein in the ledge

marks an age of water filled in with pale quartz. This bodiless wind,
its holler, perseveres—bodiless but also immoveable as a little
golden butterfly to whom air is air is air. You've grown restless

in these years away, a fair fraction of your life so far gone by—
the tip of an era's eyelash, but you never sat out here in a storm.
Woman, have you been brave? Have you been brave enough?

SHIFTING SHADOWS

Kerry W. Bernard

Shadowy waves breaking under black skies hold special magic. Never more than when draped in the full moon's glittering light. Gram taught me that. She'd take me for walks on Wells Beach long after sunset, and we'd sit and watch the moonrise from her porch.

Now, I search for glimmers of divinity in the dark alone. It sustains me through gray, dead days.

I looked extra hard in 2020. When my toes finally hit the sand on the evening of the harvest moon, the first stars had just sparked to life, and pink lingered in the west. With the tide low, the breeze still, and only a few figures dotting the blush reflected on the foreshore, the jetty called louder than usual.

But clouds blew in to swallow the remaining light, and dusk deepened into night. By the time I reached the rocks, the dark had blurred their edges too much for me to climb atop, and I worried the moon would rise behind an inky shroud. Still, I hoped for a glimpse and waited on the hard sand to see if light would conquer the disorienting dark.

I'd never known the beach to grow that black, especially so soon after sunset. Murk covered my eyes like a blindfold, sinking through my skull to fog my mind and test my balance. The shadows shifted.

I wasn't alone. Disruptions in the dark meandered around me. Other hopeful spectators of the celestial show wandered uncomfortably close, drifting silently about like ghosts. Did they not know I was there? Or did they think it was fun to haunt me?

Confusion turned to concern as two shapes sidled up—and scratched feverishly at the sand. Like werewolves, the strangers transformed into canines, the sound of digging dogs beside me unmistakable. No humans invaded my space. Only their loose pups.

Afraid of twisting an ankle in one of their holes, I retreated. I'd been too close to the jetty to see beyond it anyway, and the clouds were thinning. The dogs stayed with their holes, and the sky's downy curtains generously parted. Big and orange, the harvest moon rose like the sun, spilling its magic across the sea and sand. I tried to let some of it seep into me and forgot about the other people and their dogs.

Hoping to save a sliver of that majestic moon, I snapped a picture with my phone. To my horror, the flash went off—an ugly artificial light cutting through the sacred night.

Everything changed in that offensive burst. There were no other people. No dogs. I shared the moonrise only with a pair of foxes. They instantly fixed their glowing gazes on me, bared their fangs in devilish grins, and padded toward me as though I'd beckoned them.

For a second, I did what you're supposed to do when a wild canid comes your way—I stood my ground. Using my angriest dog-mom voice, I shouted, "No!"

They didn't so much as break stride.

I yelled again, backpedaling. "No, you stay there."

They kept coming.

Swiveling, I shoved the phone into my pocket and sprinted. Thoughts of rabies prophylaxis and appearing bloodied in a stranger's picture window rattled in my skull as my bare feet slapped the sand. Little fangs would tear into my calves at any moment. Ten seconds, fifteen seconds ... They should've caught me in five. Imagining they'd canceled the chase, I peeked over my shoulder.

The foxes trotted gleefully behind me, tongues lolling out, keeping pace. I ran hard, lungs and thighs burning, for almost half a mile before glancing back again. This time, they were gone.

I was alone.

WASHED UP

Kristen Lindquist

Alone, lying half-asleep on the beach in the fog, sleeve over my face, feeling a little sorry for myself, it's easy to imagine the osprey's cry an alarm to wake me or to express some avian concern over my inert form. But really, the bird doesn't even know I'm here, my body just one more piece of flotsam tossed among the shells and seaweed.

more than one way
to look at it

beach glass

CASTAWAYS

Marcia F. Brown

Metallic balloons have drifted away
from their parties. Morning after,
one deflated red heart
bobs in low waves. Sweet sixteen's
bright star is down to just three points.

Still, it's impossible not to be cheered
by these undulant remnants
of determined gaiety, the way they lift
and dip on the ledges, tethered
by tangles of shredded ribbon.

Even as a pewter sky forewarns
of snow, of our long winter ahead,
my pumping heart salutes
those unseen revelers, their valiant stab
at helium-lifted spirits.

These are dark days. Difficult to know
survival from ruin—mountains
of sanitized plastic to landfills, six
feet apart, we are all untouchables. Grab
-n-Go, curbside pick-up, a million ignitions

idling in parking lots. In order to live,
we've made deals with the devil. And now
these beaten globes of mylar, this
exhausted cheer too much reminds me
of all I miss—I walk on. Hearts and stars

will sink into the sea. But then I stop
and stoop to collect the glittering detritus,
pull it back from the ocean's jaws,
lest it end up in the brine-rich
deep-singing stomach

of seabird, dolphin or whale—
lest even these bits of brightness
I've grasped at as if
they might return the world to itself,
prove further our undoing.

SILVER GRAY DAY

Marjorie Arnett

A mysterious change in the air.
A dense shroud of fog moves inland.
Smell of mud, moldering leaves,
scent of approach finding its place.

It seeps through low-land shrubs,
slithers through cracks like syrup
oozing to the far side of undiscovered
crevasses lying quiet on the shore.

I write a note to a friend but my words
do not know what sentences they are in.
My thoughts are with the lift and toss
of the bay, distant sounds of ripping tides
and shadows that stir deep below the surface.

THE SOUND OF WHAT REMAINS

William Henry Forester

Not a voice,
but something close—
a hum beneath the surface of things,
woven into the breath of the tide,
the hush of pine needles shifting
on the cliffs above the bay.
It lingers in the spaces between,
in the hollowed-out places
where things have been left behind—
a forgotten dock,
a rusted chain half-buried in the sand,
the ruins of a house
no longer whole,
but not yet gone.
If you stand long enough,
where the land meets the sea,
where the fog moves slow and steady
as the hand of a clock unwinding,
you will hear it.
Not a word.
Not a cry.
Just the weight of something waiting.
Just the sound of what remains.

"We All Knew" by Lisa Tyson Ennis

ABOUT THE CONTRIBUTORS

Robin Alden has spent her career bringing fishermen's knowledge into sustainable fisheries management. She was the founding executive director of the Maine Center for Coastal Fisheries, cofounded the Maine Fishermen's Forum, and for more than twenty years published Commercial Fisheries News. She also served as Maine's commissioner of marine resources in the 1990s. She is at work on a memoir about fifty years in Maine fisheries.

Marjorie Arnett is a studio painter, playwright, and poet who served as dean of the College of Fine Arts at Indiana University of Pennsylvania. She taught painting and creative writing at the Academy of Fine Arts in Zagreb, Croatia, and held residencies in Anversa, Italy, and Porto, Portugal. She lives in Belfast, Maine. Her first poetry collection, *Ordinary Moments*, was published in 2024 by Moon Pie Press.

Ron Beard built his home in 1978 beside an abandoned granite quarry in Otter Creek on Mount Desert Island. Following his career with the University of Maine Cooperative Extension and Sea Grant, he chaired the board of the Jesup Memorial Library during a significant capital campaign and now serves as secretary of the College of the Atlantic board of trustees, where he has taught courses in community development. He credits poets Candace Stover and Leonie Charlton for encouraging his writing.

Kerry W. Bernard writes dark fantasy filled with monsters, magic, and mayhem. With a background in ecology, she is fascinated by predator-prey relationships and believes the most intense fires burn between enemies. When not working on her fiction, she enjoys roller skating, skimboarding, and spending time with her husband and daughter.

Matt Bernier lives in Belfast, Maine, where he works as a civil and environmental engineer restoring sea-run fish to Maine rivers through projects such as dam removals. His poetry has appeared in the *Maine Sunday Telegram*'s "Deep Water" column, Maine Public's *Poems from Here*, and in the anthologies *Rivers of Ink: Literary Reflections on the Penobscot River* (2023) and *North Woods at Night: Literary Reflections on Maine's Largest Forest* (2024), both published by 12 Willows Press. In 2023, he won the Maine Postmark Poetry Contest, affiliated with the Belfast Poetry Festival.

Leslie Dale Bowman has worked in the visual arts as the director of admissions at the Maine College of Art, a photographer, and a photo editor of *Bangor Metro*. She has taught on the art faculty of the University of Maine at Machias since the mid-1990s. She lives on a small saltwater farm in eastern Maine, maintaining studios for painting, clay work, and photography. Nature is her companion and inspiration.

Marcia F. Brown is the author of five poetry collections and the essay collection *Well Read, Well Fed: A Year of Great Reads and Simple Dishes for Book Groups* (Sellers Publishing, 2015). Poet Laureate of Portland, Maine, from 2013 to 2015, she edited the anthology *Port City Poems: Contemporary Poets Celebrate Portland, Maine* (Maine Poetry Council, 2013). With poet Linda Aldrich, she cohosts the Local Buzz Reading Series in Yarmouth, Maine.

Michelle Choiniere is an ESL teacher in Pittsfield, Maine. Her poems have appeared in *Vessels of Light*, *Part-time Poets*, and the anthologies *Rivers of Ink: Literary Reflections on the Penobscot River* (2023) and *North Woods at Night: Literary Reflections on Maine's Largest Forest* (2024), both published by 12 Willows Press. She is also the author and illustrator of the children's book *Cammie's Not So Normal Morning* (2024).

Erin Covey-Smith is the author of *Not-Yet Elegies* (Finishing Line Press, 2020). Her award-winning poetry appears in anthologies and journals including *kerning*, *humana obscura*, *Rust & Moth*, and *Third Wednesday*. She holds an MFA in printmaking from Concordia University and has pursued both visual and written artistic practices throughout her career. She lives in Freeport, Maine.

Betty Culley is the author of poetry, young adult verse novels, and middle-grade fiction. Her YA novels in verse include *Three Things I Know Are True* (HarperCollins, 2020) and *The Name She Gave Me* (HarperCollins, 2022). Her middle-grade novels include *Down to Earth* (Crown Books, 2021) and *The Natural Genius of Ants* (Crown Books, 2022). Her next book, *Landslide*, will be published in March 2026 by Nancy Paulsen Books. She lives in central Maine.

Nancy Dewey is a third-generation traditional photographer whose work centers on documentary, portraiture, and nature. A former darkroom technician, she began with black-and-white film before moving into digital practice. Her exhibits include *Journeys*, *Rural Community and Change*, *Fathers*, *Elder Artists*, and *Life Perspective*. In 2013, she self-published *Tinta*, a trilingual photographic essay of the Peruvian altiplano.

Kara Douglas is a writer, teacher, and small business owner in Harpswell, Maine, with her husband and two daughters. She teaches yoga and meditation in the renovated hayloft of their early 1900s barn. For eleven years, she wrote monthly articles for *The Harpswell Anchor*. Her work has appeared in several anthologies, including *Balancing Act 2: An Anthology of Poems by Fifty Maine Women* (Littoral Books, 2018), *Wait: Poems from the Pandemic* (Littoral Books, 2021), *Rivers of Ink: Literary Reflections on the Penobscot* (12 Willows Press, 2023), and *Writing the Land: Maine* (2022) and *Writing the Land: Maine II, A Gathering* (2024), both published by NatureCulture LLC. Kara coedited and contributed to *Alive to This: Essays on Living Fully by 20 Maine Writers* (Littoral Books, 2024).

Rick Doyle is a poet and playwright and works as a staff attorney at a non-profit providing civil legal representation to survivors of domestic violence. He lives in Bucksport, Maine.

Susan Doyle grew up in the Midwest but has long been drawn to the ocean. In retirement, she devotes herself to reading and writing poetry, gardening, and keeping deer and porcupines out of her vegetable and flower beds. She lives with her husband and their cat, who helps keep her sense of humor alive.

Karen Egee lives in Maine with her husband and dog. A retired child psychologist, she writes creative nonfiction and takes photographs to savor the good and make sense of the rest. Her work has appeared in *Unbroken Journal*, the *Brevity* podcast, and Passager's *Pandemic Diaries*.

Kathleen Ellis's poetry collections include *Red Horses* (Northern Lights, 1991), (with R. W. Estela) *Narrow River to the North: Poems & Prose of the Penobscot Watershed* (Amapola Books, 2011), and *Body of Evidence* (Grayson Books, 2023). Her poems have appeared in *The Café Review, Rumors, Secrets, and Lies, A Dangerous New World: Maine Voices on the Climate Crisis* (Littoral Books, 2019), and *Rivers of Ink: Literary Reflections on the Penobscot* (12 Willows Press, 2023). Poetry from her manuscript "Dear Darwin" was set to music for a Parma Recordings CD, nominated for a 2015 Grammy Award. Kathleen teaches creative writing at the University of Maine and lives on Marsh Island in Orono.

Lisa Tyson Ennis has photographed the Maine coast for many years, working in both digital formats and historic photographic processes. Several fine art galleries in Maine represent her work. She lives year-round in Blue Hill with her husband, dog, and cat.

Gro Flatebo earned an MFA from the Stonecoast program after a career of more than twenty-five years in the environmental field. She has attended the Bread Loaf Writers' Conferences, Atlantic Center for the Arts residencies, and the Vermont Studio Center. A former nonfiction editor for *Fifth Wednesday Journal*, her work has appeared in *South Dakota Review, New Madrid Journal, Avalon Literary Review, Platte Valley Review, Hunger Mountain*'s "Loose Sally" blog, *Boston Literary Magazine*, and *The Collagist*. She has lived on the Maine coast for forty years.

Richard Foerster is the author of nine poetry collections, most recently *With Little Light and Sometimes None at All* (Littoral Books, 2023), which received a Gold Medal at the 2024 Independent Publishers of New England Book Awards. His honors include the "Discovery"/*The Nation* Award, *Poetry* magazine's Bess Hokin Prize, the Amy Lowell Poetry Travelling Scholarship, two National Endowment for the Arts Poetry Fellowships, and two Maine Literary Awards for Poetry. His work has appeared in *The Best American Poetry*, *Kenyon Review*, *TriQuarterly*, *The Gettysburg Review*, *Boulevard*, *The Southern Review*, and *Poetry*. He lives in Eliot, Maine.

William Henry Forester is a poet, folklorist, and storyteller whose work explores the intersections of memory, myth, and the sea. Born in Inverness in the Scottish Highlands, he now lives on the Maine coast with his wife. His writing ranges from poetry and children's tales to coastal mysteries, often reflecting themes of solitude, loss, and the echoes of what we leave behind.

Jay Franzel lives in Wayne, Maine, and likes to travel with his dog. He organizes The Bookey Readings, the longest-running poetry series in Maine, currently held at Bailey Library in Winthrop.

Hank Garfield grew up on Maine's Blue Hill Peninsula and is the author of five novels. He teaches English and creative writing at the University of Maine and has also taught at Palomar College in California, Eastern Maine Community College, and the American University in Bulgaria. His nonfiction book *Slower Traffic: Life without a Car in Maine, USA* is to be published by 12 Willows Press in 2027.

Ellen Goldsmith reads, writes, and teaches poetry. Her most recent book, *Left Foot, Right Foot* (2021), is a collection of poems about illness and recovery. Other chapbooks include *No Pine Tree in This Forest Is Perfect* (Slapering Hol Press, 1997), *Such Distances* (2009), and *Where to Look* (2013). Her poems have appeared in numerous journals and anthologies. She holds an EdD from Columbia University and is a professor emerita at The City University of New York. She lives in Cushing, Maine.

Melodie Prescott Greene was born and raised in Maine and earned a doctorate in psychology from the University of Maine at Orono. Her work has appeared in *The Binnacle*, the Eastport Arts Center's "Life in Washington County" series, and local histories. Her short story collection, *Eddie and Me, Romancing the Wild Maine Woods,* was published in 2024 by Sea Smoke

Press. In 2020, she received Honorable Mention in *Writer's Digest*'s Memoirs/Personal Essay category.

Andrea Suarez Hill is a New England native who has lived in Jonesboro, Maine, for thirty-eight years, following a career in print, broadcast, and photojournalism in New York City. Her poetry has appeared in *The Aurorean*, *3 Nations Anthology: Native, Canadian & New England Writers* (Resolute Bear Press, 2017), *A Dangerous New World: Maine Voices on the Climate Crisis* (Littoral Books, 2019), and other journals and anthologies. She is the author of *The Making of Budworm Farm* (Goose River Press, 2020) and *A Portrait to Paint* (Austin Macauley, 2023).

Annaliese Jakimides's work has appeared in print, audio, exhibit, and performance venues nationally and internationally. Nominated for Pushcart Prizes and Best of the Nets, she's been a finalist for many awards, including the Stephen Dunn Poetry Prize and Maine Literary Awards in multiple genres in multiple years. Her poetry and prose have appeared in many magazines (*Utne, GQ*), journals (*Beloit, Consequence*), and anthologies (Beacon Press, Golden Books, Seal Press, Henry Holt, Littoral Books, 12 Willows Press, and more). Broadcast on Maine Public and NPR, she's a freelance writer, editor, and facilitator who's worked with environmental justice organizations, international arts groups, and people in prisons. After decades in the woods of northern Maine, she lives in Bangor. annaliesejakimides.com and @annaliese_jakimides

Kate Kearns is the author of *You Are Ruining My Loneliness* (Littoral Books, 2023) and *How to Love an Introvert* (Finishing Line Press, 2015). Her work has appeared in *Maine Women Magazine, Rustica*, the *Maine Sunday Telegram*'s "Deep Water" column, Maine Public's *Poems from Here*, *Salamander, Peregrine, Sugar House Review*, and elsewhere. A finalist for the Charles Simic Memorial Prize and the 2024 Maine Postmark Poetry Contest, she earned her MFA from Lesley University. katekearns.com

Shir Kehila is a freelance writer, editor, and translator based on Mount Desert Island. Her work has appeared or is forthcoming in *Off Assignment*,

Majuscule, *Indiana Review*, *Here for All the Reasons* (Turner Publishing, 2026), and other publications. She holds an MFA from Columbia University and has received scholarships from the Bread Loaf Writers' Conference, the Tin House Summer Workshop, and the Monson Arts Residency.

Dan Kirchoff is an artist and illustrator, living with his wife, Jen, and three cats in Belfast, Maine. He earned a BFA from Auburn University in 1983 and worked as a project coordinator and book designer for a midcoast Maine division of McGraw-Hill for eleven years, totaling over forty years in books and newspapers. Kirchoff creates pen-and-ink portraiture and local scenes, political cartoons for *The Midcoast Villager*, and acrylic Maine landscapes and still lifes, which he shows locally. dankirchoff.com

Hans Krichels is a teacher, writer, woodcarver, and grandfather who has lived and worked in Bucksport, Maine, since 1971. His recent work appears in *Goose River Anthology, 2020* (Goose River Press, 2020), *Rivers of Ink: Literary Reflections on the Penobscot* (12 Willows Press, 2023), *Willie Knows Who Done It* (Atmosphere Press, 2020) and *We Have Met the Enemy: Stories and Other Writings from the Days of Pandemic in My Town* (Maine Authors Publishing, 2021), among others. hanskrichels.com

Jennie Kuhn grew up in the suburbs of Philadelphia and now makes her home in Maine with her spouse, Tracy, their dog, Wesley, and several well-loved cats. She studied English and creative writing at Ursinus College and recently earned her MS in clinical mental health counseling from Husson University. She writes poetry, though she says poems often write themselves.

faith lane is a poet, author, librarian, genealogist, and adventurer. She has been writing poetry since age eight and studying genealogy since age nine. faith has published five books, including *toxic & tonic* (2022) and *lighthouses of midcoast maine & tales of the folk who lived there* (2024). She lives in Downeast Maine with her husband, where their herb gardens and meadows provide a home for birds, bees, butterflies, and other wild creatures.

Andrea Lani is a book coach, freelance writer, and the author of *Uphill Both Ways: Hiking toward Happiness on the Colorado Trail* (Bison Books, 2022). Her work has appeared in *Still Point Arts Quarterly*, *The Maine Review*, *Northern Woodlands*, and other publications. She holds a BA in human ecology from the College of the Atlantic and an MFA in creative writing from Stonecoast. She teaches nature writing and nature journaling workshops throughout Maine. andrealani.com and andreaelani.substack.com

Valerie Lawson has published work in *Café Review*, *About Place Journal*, *The Catch*, *Maine Farms*, and other outlets. She participated in the Writing the Land project, connecting poets with protected spaces. Before moving to Maine in 2007, she was part of the Boston Poetry Slam and Doc Brown's Traveling Poetry Show. Valerie coedited *Off the Coast* literary journal and edited *3 Nations Anthology: Native, Canadian & New England Writers* (Resolute Bear Press), winner of the Maine Literary Award.

Catherine J.S. Lee continues to celebrate her Downeast Maine home in stories, poems, and photographs. An almost-lifelong island resident familiar with coastal fog, she began writing in first grade and published her first piece at age eight. Her newest collection, *A Place to Land: More Stories from the Coast of Maine*, was published by Sea Smoke Press in 2025, following her award-winning *Island Secrets: Stories from the Coast of Maine* (Sea Smoke Press, 2022).

Erine Leigh lives in Eastport, Maine. She is a former poet laureate of Portsmouth, New Hampshire.

Kristen Lindquist has published work in *Down East Magazine*, *Pen Bay Pilot*, *Bangor Daily News*, and numerous literary journals and anthologies. Her poetry collection, *Transportation* (Megunticook Press, 2011), was a finalist for the Maine Literary Award. Her most recent books are *Tourists in the Known World: New & Selected Poems* (Megunticook Press, 2017) and *Island* (Red Moon Press, 2023), an award-winning haiku collection. She divides her time between Monhegan Island and Camden, Maine.

Carl Little is the author of *Blanket of the Night: Poems* (Deerbrook Editions, 2024) and *Ocean Drinker: New & Selected Poems* (Deerbrook Editions, 2006). His poems have appeared in *The Café Review*, *Maine Arts Journal*, *Maine Sunday Telegram*, and other publications, as well as in several anthologies edited by Wesley McNair. In 2021, the Rabkin Foundation presented him with a Lifetime Achievement Award for his art writing. He lives on Mount Desert Island.

JK McGann spent many years in the arid Southwest working on ecology projects before returning to the ocean she missed. An occasional contributor to scientific journals, she now turns her focus to poetry inspired by the Maine coast.

Cathy McKelway writes middle-grade and young-adult fiction. Her short story "The Survey" won the YA Review Network's 2017 Halloween contest. She has also placed in Rate Your Story's Awesome Openings contest and received an honorable mention for her YA ghost novel. She occasionally writes adult flash fiction. Cathy lives in her grandmother's house in the Maine woods. cathymckelway.com

Brook Merrow has taught writing at the middle school, high school, and college levels. She is the author of *Trapped* (Maine Authors Publishing, 2023), a young-adult novel set on the Maine coast. She enjoys irreverent humor, a twist of irony, and all kinds of exercise.

Leslie Moore is a poet and printmaker whose work often focuses on animals. She is the author and illustrator of *Grackledom* (Littoral Books, 2023) and *What Rough Beasts* (Littoral Books, 2021), and winner of the 2018 Maine Literary Award for Short Nonfiction. Her poems and essays have appeared in *The Maine Standard*, *Poems from Here*, *Spire: The Maine Journal of Conservation and Sustainability*, *Deep Water*, and *Rivers of Ink: Literary Reflections on the Penobscot* (12 Willows Press, 2023). Her artwork is found in book illustrations, private collections, the Local Color Gallery in Belfast, and the Wendell Gilley Museum in Southwest Harbor.

Jefferson Navicky is the author of four books, most recently *Head of Island Beautification for the Rural Outlands* (AC Books, 2023), a finalist for the Big Other Book Award in Fiction, and *Antique Densities: Modern Parables & Other Experiments in Short Prose* (Deerbrook Editions, 2021), winner of the Maine Literary Award for Poetry. He is the archivist for the Maine Women Writers Collection and lives in Midcoast Maine.

Amanda Neitz is a geomorphologist, musician, member of the Order of Bards, Ovates, and Druids, and mother. She lives within the alchemy where science and art meet.

Nandiya Nyx is a poet, photographer, and interpreter living in Portland, Maine. She often walks to the water's edge near her home, where she finds sanctuary and inspiration for poems. Her work has appeared in *Just This Zen*, *Sinister Wisdom*, and the *Poetry Marathon Anthology* (Authors Publish Press, 2021-2024), among other publications.

Christopher Packard is a science teacher, folklorist, and storyteller based in the Greater Bangor area. He is the assistant director of the International Cryptozoology Museum and the author of *Mythical Creatures of Maine: Fantastic Beasts from Legend and Folklore* (Down East Books, 2021) and the children's book *Lumpy's Gift* (12 Willows Press, 2023). christopherpackard.com

Donald M. Peterson is a photographer and mixed media artist living on the Maine coast. A licensed architect, he has spent fifty years in architecture, urban planning, and real estate development while pursuing a self-directed creative education. Over the past decade, he has focused increasingly on painting and photography, with work exhibited in galleries from Maine to South Carolina and collected throughout the United States.

Deborah Pfeffer is a Maine-based writer whose work explores poetry, dreams, and quiet stories. Her award-winning essay "Christmas on the Hard" appeared in *Kaleidoscope*. Her poetry has been published in *Chorale* (Deer Brook Editions, 2022) and *Persimmon Tree*. She continues to write from the inspiration of the natural world as she completes *Mates*, a personal narrative of a four-year journey aboard her sailboat, *Piper*.

Gary Rainford lives year-round on an island off Maine's northeast coast. His third book, *Adrift*, tells the stories of his mother's dementia and Alzheimer's disease and was a 2022 finalist for the Independent Publishers of New England Poetry Award. garyrainford.com.

Patricia Smith Ranzoni is Poet Laureate Emerita of Bucksport, Maine (2014–2025), where she grew up. Her work has appeared in the *Portland Press Herald*'s "Deep Water" column and the 12 Willows Press anthologies *Rivers of Ink: Literary Reflections on the Penobscot* and *North Woods at Night: Literary Reflections on Maine's Largest Forest*. Her poems have also been featured on Maine Public Radio and Maine Public Classical's "Poems From Here," read by Maine Poet Laureate Julia Bouwsma.

Cynthia Reeves is the author of *The Last Whaler* and *Falling Through the New World*—both Foreword INDIES finalists—and *Badlands*, winner of the Miami University Press Novella Prize. Her poetry and fiction have appeared widely, and she has held residencies with the Arctic Circle, Hawthornden Castle, and the Vermont Studio Center. A graduate of the Warren Wilson MFA program, she has taught at Bryn Mawr and Rosemont College. Now living in Camden, Maine, she draws inspiration from the landscapes of her youth, exploring themes of memory, place, and environmental loss.

John Reinhart is the winner of the Horror Writers Association Dark Poetry Scholarship and former editor of *Star*Line*. His poetry ranges from heartfelt to heart-wrenching to robots in space with no hearts. He also manages *Poetry Across Maine*, an oral history and documentary self-guided tour of Maine through poetry. home.hampshire.edu/~jcr00/reinhart.html

Catherine Schmitt is a science writer and the author of nonfiction books, including *A Coastal Companion: A Year in the Gulf of Maine from Cape Cod to Canada* (Tilbury House, 2008) and the forthcoming *Trees of Acadia* (Down East, 2026). catherineschmitt.com

Nomar Slevik is an independent writer, researcher, and investigator of the paranormal. His lifelong passion is to explore and share otherworldly encounters in ways that emphasize the human experience at the heart of the strange and unexplained.

K. Stephens is an award-winning Maine journalist and author of *The Ghost Trap*, adapted into an independent feature film in 2024. Of Irish descent, she traveled extensively through Ireland, Scotland, and England to collect selkie folklore, spending ten years writing the novel. She lives in Midcoast Maine.

Marianne Stratton lives with her wife and children in an 1840s New Englander near the Penobscot River, with a glimpse of the water when the trees are bare. First published in *Earth's Daughters* in 1997 and later in *Lilliput Review* and other journals, she has returned to submitting her work after years away and continues to write toward the mermaid grotto at the end of the path.

Kathleen Sullivan is a writer, climate activist, and clinical social worker with five decades of practice. Since 2020, she has written a weekly Substack blog—first *Process Notes of a Pandemic*, then *Code Red and Me: Rethinking Everything*, and now *Code Red: Process Notes of a Coup*. Her work has appeared in several Littoral Books anthologies and other publications. She is the founder and coordinator of Freeport Climate Action Now. Originally from a small working-class town on Long Island's South Shore, she now lives a mile from the ocean in Freeport, Maine.

Ret Talbot is an award-winning independent journalist and writer who covers ocean issues and animals at the intersection of science and sustainability. His work can be found in publications such as *Discover Magazine, National Geographic, Mongabay,* and *Yale Environment 360*. His most recent book, *Chasing Shadows: My Life Tracking the Great White Shark* (William Morrow, 2023), co-written with shark biologist Greg Skomal, is a conservation success story about restoring an apex predator to an ecosystem. Ret lives on the coast of Maine with his wife, scientific illustrator Karen Talbot.

Greg Westrich spent much of his adult life traveling before settling in Maine. He is the author of a dozen Falcon hiking guides and has written for *Down East, Canoe & Kayak, Bird Watching*, and other publications. He frequently gives talks and slide show presentations at libraries and for outing clubs. He teaches writing and literature at Deer Isle/Stonington High School. He is the creator of Maine's Wicked Wild 25 hiking list. gregwestrich.com

Douglas Wright is an aspiring writer living in the countryside of Downeast Maine.

INDEX - CONTRIBUTORS

INDEX - SELECTIONS

POETRY